P9-DHJ-050

HOWLIDAY INN

Pinky and Rex Series
Pinky and Rex
*Pinky and Rex Get
    Married*
*Pinky and Rex and the
    Mean Old Witch*
*Pinky and Rex and the
    Spelling Bee*
*Pinky and Rex Go to
    Camp*
*Pinky and Rex and the
    New Baby*
*Pinky and Rex and the
    Double-Dad Weekend*
*Pinky and Rex and the
    Bully*
*Pinky and Rex and the
    New Neighbors*
*Pinky and Rex and the
    Perfect Pumpkin*
*Pinky and Rex and the
    School Play*
*Pinky and Rex and the
    Just-Right Pet*

Novels
A Night Without Stars
Morgan's Zoo
The Watcher
The Misfits
Totally Joe

**Edited by
    James Howe**
*The Color of Absence:
    Twelve Stories about
    Loss and Hope*
*13: Thirteen Stories
    That Capture the Agony
    and Ecstasy of Being
    Thirteen*

HOWLIDAY INN

by JAMES HOWE

ILLUSTRATED BY LYNN MUNSINGER

ATHENEUM BOOKS FOR YOUNG READERS
New York London Toronto Sydney

In memory of
Debbie

If you purchased this book without a cover, you should be aware that this book is stolen property. It was reported as "unsold and destroyed" to the publisher, and neither the author nor the publisher has received any payment for this "stripped book."

ATHENEUM BOOKS FOR YOUNG READERS
An imprint of Simon & Schuster Children's Publishing Division
1230 Avenue of the Americas, New York, New York 10020
This book is a work of fiction. Any references to historical events, real people, or real locales are used fictitiously. Other names, characters, places, and incidents are products of the author's imagination, and any resemblance to actual events or locales or persons, living or dead, is entirely coincidental.
Text copyright © 1982 by James Howe
Illustrations copyright © 1982 by Simon & Schuster, Inc.
All rights reserved, including the right of reproduction in whole or in part in any form.
ATHENEUM BOOKS FOR YOUNG READERS is a registered trademark of
Simon & Schuster, Inc.
For information about special discounts for bulk purchases, please contact
Simon & Schuster Special Sales at 1-866-506-1949 or business@simonandschuster.com.
The Simon & Schuster Speakers Bureau can bring authors to your live event. For more information or to book an event, contact the Simon & Schuster Speakers Bureau at
1-866-248-3049 or visit our website at www.simonspeakers.com.
Also available in a hardcover edition.
Book design by Mary A. Ahern
Manufactured in the United States of America
0718 OFF
First paperback edition September 2001
20 19
The Library of Congress has cataloged the hardcover edition as follows:
Howe, James. Howliday Inn.
Summary: While their family is away, Harold and Chester, a dog and cat, are boarded at Chateau Bow-Wow, where Chester becomes increasingly alarmed by the strange behavior of his fellow guests and the sudden disappearance of one of them.
[1. Cats—Fiction. 2. Dogs—Fiction. 3. Mystery and detective stories.]
I. Munsinger, Lynn. II. Title.
PZ7.H8372Ho [Fic]   81-10886
ISBN 978-0-689-30846-8 (hc)
ISBN 978-1-4169-2815-7 (pbk)
ISBN 978-1-4424-5210-7 (eBook)

EDITOR'S NOTE

I HAD THOUGHT I'd heard the last of Harold, the writing dog, when he delivered his book, *Bunnicula,* to my office some time ago. Much to my surprise, he suddenly appeared again one recent rainy Wednesday afternoon. The dreary weather had made the day useless for anything more than catching up on all those boring little chores one puts off for just such days and drinking a lot of reheated coffee to cut the constant chill that sneaks in through the cracks in the windows. When I heard scratching at my door, I thought it was probably a stray cat looking for a warm radiator and a saucer of milk. That alone, I reasoned, would provide some relief from the monotony of the day's non-events.

You can well imagine my delight when I opened the door and saw Harold standing on the other side of the portal, his hair drenched and hanging from him like an unwrung mop. From his teeth dangled a plastic bag. I asked him in and examined the contents of the bag that he'd dropped at my feet. What I found was the manuscript of Harold's new book, together with this note:

My dear colleague,
I had not planned to write again. Indeed, after my friend Chester read my first book, he accused me of writing without a literary license. I had settled into my comfortable life as a nice American middle-class dog with my nice American middle-class family when strange events once again engulfed me. Naturally, after all the fur had flown and the dust had settled, I felt compelled to write the story down.

What resulted is the manuscript you now see before you. I do hope you will enjoy it and, as before, find it worthy of your readers' attentions.

Your humble servant,
Harold X.

I convinced Harold to stay long enough for a doughnut and a bowl of hot chocolate. Then, as suddenly as he'd appeared, he was gone, leaving behind him the pages of his story, which he has chosen to call *Howliday Inn*.

Contents

HOWLIDAY INN

ONE

The Departure

LOOKING back on it now, I doubt that there was any way I could have imagined what lay ahead. After all, I'm not as well read as Chester, and except for the time I'd run away from home as a puppy and spent a fitful night under a neighbor's Porsche, I really had had very little experience of my own in the outside world. How could I have begun to imagine then what would befall me that fateful week in August?

If the memories of that week no longer make my blood run cold, they still have enough of a chilling effect to give me pause. Why, you may wonder, do I wish to stir them up now when I could so easily curl up in front of a nice warm radiator and think of happier times instead? The answer, a simple one really, is just this: whatever else may be said of that week, it was an adventure. And adventures, no matter how dark or disturbing to recall, are meant to be shared.

IT BEGAN innocently enough on a beautiful summer's day, the kind of day, I remember thinking, when the universe seems in perfect order and nothing can go wrong. A soft breeze ruffled the hairs along my neck. Birds chirped happily in the trees. A butterfly landed on my nose and would have stayed for a while, I think, if I hadn't sneezed him off. The sky was blue, the sun was gold, the grass was green. Such riches cannot be bought for any price, I thought, as I lay stretched out on the front lawn chewing contentedly on one of Mr. Monroe's new running shoes.

Without warning, my blissful mood was shattered by the sound of Toby's voice coming from within the house.

"Why?" he kept repeating, a bit unpleasantly.

His mother answered him in that ever-patient

way of hers. "You've asked me several times, Toby, and I keep telling you the same thing. I know you're not happy about it, but we can't take them with us."

"But why? Why?" Toby insisted loudly. I noticed several butterflies flutter away from our yard defensively. "We've taken Harold and Chester on vacation with us before," he whined. My ears perked up. *I* was the topic of discussion.

"Just to the lake house, Toby, never on a car trip," Mrs. Monroe answered. "There won't be room. Besides, you know Harold gets carsick. You wouldn't want him to be miserable, would you?"

"No," Toby agreed sensibly, "I guess you're right."

Darn right she is, I thought.

"But I'm going to miss them, Mom," Toby added.

Mrs. Monroe's voice softened. "I know you are, Toby. We'll all miss them. But we'll be gone only a week, and then we'll see them again. Think of everything you'll have to tell Harold when you get home."

"Yeah, I guess so," Toby said, his voice trailing off in defeat. Poor kid, I thought, he's really broken up. Well, I couldn't blame him. I *was* a lot of fun, after all, and it was natural he'd want to take me along. I mean, who would he play fetch-the-stick with? Whose tummy would he rub?

Suddenly, panic seized me. Who was going to feed us? I dropped my Adidas, moved quickly to the front door and began scratching on the screen.

"Hi, Harold," Toby said as he let me in. He looked at me sadly and put his arms around my neck. "I'm sorry, boy. Mom says we can't take you on vacation this time. I'll bet you feel real disappointed, huh?"

Who's going to feed me? I asked with my eyes.

"But don't worry. We'll be back in a week. It won't be so long. Still, you feel bad you're not going, don't you? I know."

Who's going to feed me? I pleaded, with a hint of a whimper.

"Oh, and if you're wondering what's going to happen to you while we're away . . ."

Yes? I asked, my eyes growing wider.

". . . don't worry. Mom and Dad have that all figured out. See, Bunnicula is going to stay next door at Professor Mickelwhite's house . . ." I glanced over at the windowsill where the rabbit's cage was kept and saw that it had already been removed. I felt myself breaking into a cold sweat. What was going to happen to *me?* ". . . and you and Chester are going to be boarded."

Oh, I thought, feeling relieved immediately, that's all right then. Just one little detail troubled me: I didn't have the slightest idea what being boarded meant. I decided to find Chester and ask him about it, since Chester knows, or thinks he knows, something about almost everything.

When I found him, he was sitting in the back yard staring off into space. Chester, being a cat, is very good at staring off into space. He once explained to me that this was his way of meditating or, as he liked to put it, "getting mellow." At the moment I found him, he looked so mellow I thought there was a good chance of his ripening and rotting right there before my eyes if I didn't shake him out of it quickly.

"The Monroes are leaving, and they're going to do something to us with boards," I told him.

"Don't say hello or anything," Chester replied, without moving a muscle.

"Oh, sorry. Hello, Chester. How's it going?"

Chester just nodded his head slowly as if that were supposed to be telling me something. "Now what was that about boards?" he asked at last.

"I'm not sure. They're leaving, and they're going to tie us to boards or something, that's all I know."

"I'm sure that's not *all* you know, Harold," he said smoothly. "It may be all your brain can handle right now, but I'm sure you know at least one or two things more. Now, let's try again. What exactly did you hear?"

"Well," I explained, "Toby told me that while the family goes on vacation, you and I are going to be boarded."

"Boarded?!!" Chester exclaimed, his mellowness suddenly gone with the passing breeze. "We're going to be boarded? I can't believe they'd do this to us. It figures! That's all I can say. It just figures!"

"What figures?" I asked. "What are they going to do to us?"

"Oh, just lock us up and throw away the key, that's all. Prison, Harold, that's what it boils down to. We're in their way now that they want to go off and have some fun. So out the door we go and into some dank, dark pit where we'll be fed moldy bread and rainwater—*if* we're lucky! You don't know what these places are like, Harold. But I do!"

"How?" I asked. "Were you ever boarded?"

"Was I ever *boarded?* Was *I* ever boarded?"

"That's what I asked, Chester. Were you ever boarded?"

"*I*'ve read Charles Dickens, sport," was his only reply, and he turned his attention to his tail, which he suddenly felt compelled to bathe. A scowl grew on his face, and I thought that if it were possible, dark rain clouds would have formed around his eyebrows.

"I'll tell you something else, Harold," he muttered. His hysteria had subsided, and he spoke now in a low, serious tone.

"What's that?"

"You have to keep your eyes open all the time in places like those. You never know what will happen next."

"What do you mean?" I asked.

"Think about it," he went on. "A group of strangers are thrown together by circumstance. Who knows who they are? Where they've come from? What they're doing there? The one smiling at you across the food dish in the morning could murder you in your sleep at night."

"Chester," I said, interrupting, "I think perhaps your imagination is running away with you."

"Hah!" Chester snorted. "Mark my words, Harold. Keep your eyes open and your door shut. Just remember: they aren't called strangers for nothing!" And he walked away, leaving me alone with my thoughts.

With everything Chester had said about strangers, it was hard for me at that moment to picture anyone stranger than Chester. But time would certainly bear out his warning. And I have to admit that even then there was something in the conviction with which he spoke that made me uneasy. So much so that when I saw Mr. Monroe coming in my direction, I was immediately distrustful. And this of a man whose home I had lived in for years and whose running shoes I had been eating but moments before!

"Hey there, Harold, guess what? You're going away on a little vacation. Aren't you lucky?" I smelled a con job and kept my distance. "You and Chester are going to stay in a nice animal hotel for a few days. You'll meet some new friends and have a lot of fun. Doesn't that sound terrific?" Interesting he doesn't mention the food, I thought. Having no intention of being conned into living on mold and rainwater, I decided to try a tactic I save for only the most dire of circumstances. As pitifully as I knew how, I started to whimper.

"Aw, poor Harold," Mr. Monroe said quietly, reaching down to pat me on the top of my head (I was sure I had him hooked), "I wish we could take you with us, fella, but we can't." Rats. "Besides, you'll have a good time at Chateau Bow-Wow. Doesn't that sound like a nice place to stay? Now, come on, boy," he said, moving back toward the driveway, "jump up here into the back of the station wagon."

Hmm, Chateau Bow-Wow, I thought as I followed him, it doesn't sound so bad. Not the Waldorf-Astoria maybe, but not bad. Still, I wasn't sure I wanted to go anywhere, particularly after everything Chester had just told me. I lifted my head and let out a soft, muted moan. When I dropped my head again, I noticed Chester lying under the car in the shade by the rear tire. He looked at me and shook his head slowly.

"What a disgusting display," he said, sighing heavily. "But what can one expect from a dog, after all?"

"Well," I replied, "I'm glad to see that you're so resigned to being dragged off to prison."

"I'm not resigned," he said calmly, licking a paw. "I'm not going."

"Oh really?" I asked. "And just how do you intend to manage that?"

Before he could answer, Mrs. Monroe came out of the front door with Chester's carrier, a large square box with a little window in one end. I always tell Chester that it looks like he's on television when he's inside. He doesn't find that very amusing. In fact, just the sight of his carrier is usually enough to send him into a panic, hissing and hyperventilating up a storm. This time, however, he seemed determined to remain cool.

"Toby," Mrs. Monroe instructed her youngest son, "see if you and Pete can find Chester, will you?" Pete appeared at the door behind Toby.

"Excuse me," Chester said to me, "it's time for my exit." And so saying, he made a mad dash for the nearest lilac bush.

Unfortunately for him, Toby and Pete were on to his favorite hiding places. And Pete, who had taken up jogging with his dad, was fast on Chester's heels. Grabbing him by the tail (not the best place to grab anyone, let alone a cat), Pete yanked him back and into his arms before Chester could do much more than let out a yelp of disapproval. Pete then attempted to force

Chester into the waiting carrier, but Chester spread out all four of his legs so that his paws tightly clamped the edges of the box. With his legs held rigidly in place, he screamed and he hissed and he generally let it be known in no uncertain terms that he had no intention of going anywhere. All, however, was to no avail, for he was quickly surrounded by the entire Monroe family, and before he knew what had happened, he was squashed into the carrier and plopped into the car.

I, on the other hand, went with quiet dignity, allowing myself to be lured into the back of the station wagon by a chocolate cupcake and Mr. Monroe's calm affirmation that adventure was good for the soul.

Chester and I had a few moments alone before the rest of the family joined us. Licking the last traces of chocolate frosting from the tip of my nose, I turned to the beast growling inside the cat carrier. I was intrigued by Mr. Monroe's statement about the effect of adventure on the soul and thought perhaps I could pass the time engaging Chester in a deep philosophical conversation.

"Well, Chester," I began, "what do *you* think?"

"I think you made a fool of yourself over that cupcake," he said.

Then again, I thought, perhaps not. I decided to try another tack.

"You know, Chester," I said, trying to sound cheerful, "maybe there's nothing for us to worry about. The way Mr. Monroe tells it, Chateau Bow-Wow sounds like a really nice place."

Chester, who had been grumbling under his breath all this time, was suddenly silent.

"What did you say?" he asked after a moment.

"I said, 'Chateau Bow-Wow sounds like a really nice place.'"

"Chateau Bow-Wow?"

"Chateau Bow-Wow."

Chester's face appeared in the window. His eyes were gleaming.

"What's the problem?" I asked.

"Oh, there's no problem, Harold. No problem at all. Just because I'm being forced to spend a week of my life in a place obviously run by dog chauvinists who are totally insensitive to my feline feelings! Why should that bother me? No, I don't have a problem, Harold. It's the rest of the world who have the problems!"

"Gee, you know, Chester," I said to him, "you look just like a guest on a talk show."

"Harold, have you heard one word I've said?"

"Chester, could you pretend you're on a talk show? You know—just say, 'Gee, it's swell to be here today, Merv,' or 'Well, you know, Mike, it's funny you should ask about that. . . .' Okay, Chester? Huh? Sing 'Feelings,' okay? Chester? Chester?"

Chester glared at me and dropped out of sight. I heard him muttering something about dogs, but I couldn't understand what he was saying. I stopped trying after the Monroes had gotten into the car and I noticed we were pulling out of the driveway.

There was a rumble of thunder in the distance as the car went over a bump and my stomach lurched. Why, I asked myself, had I eaten that chocolate cupcake? I closed my eyes and gritted my teeth.

Toby and Pete were fighting about who had the best window. Mrs. Monroe was trying to quiet them down, at the same time pointing out to Mr. Monroe that he had just taken a wrong turn. Chester, meanwhile, was grumbling and hissing inside his carrier. "Mark my words, Harold," I heard him say at one point, "there's trouble ahead. Don't say I didn't warn you."

As I was thinking back on the feelings of peace and contentment with which I'd started the day, Mr. Monroe turned up the volume on the radio. ". . . so the outlook for the rest of the week," the announcer was saying, "is heavy rain and thunderstorms."

Everyone groaned. The car hit another bump, and my stomach began to feel like a washing machine on the spin cycle. This adventure, I thought, may be terrific for my soul, but it's going to wreak havoc on my digestive system.

TWO

Welcome to
Howliday Inn

THERE was something about Chateau Bow-Wow that made me uncomfortable from the moment I saw it. Sitting alone on the top of a hill, it inspired a feeling of desolation. Of course, the bumpy ride up the long, winding country road that led to it inspired a feeling of upset tummy, but that's another story.

"Where are we?" I asked in a hushed whisper. I had never seen this part of town before.

"No man's land," Chester growled reassuringly from the bottom of his box.

A second low rumble of thunder resounded in

the distance, and then as we pulled into the driveway, I became aware of another sound.

"Do you hear all that barking?" I asked Chester.
A chill went through me.

Together, we listened for a moment. Then
Chester spoke. "No doubt the victims of some
fiendish laboratory experiment," he said.

I gulped.

"Well, this is the place," Mr. Monroe called
back cheerily from the front seat as he brought
the car to a halt. "You two stay put. We'll be
right back." And all the Monroes went off through
a door marked "Office" to do whatever it is people
do in offices.

Not to mince words, I was petrified. Where
were the Monroes leaving us, anyway? Boy, I
thought, you trust some people, you give them
the best years of your life, and what does it get
you? Abandonment and despair. A fine kettle of
fish, that's what I had to say.

I looked around after a moment. The place
didn't seem quite so bad close up. I suppose it was
the sign that helped most. It was on the gate of a

wall behind the house, and when I saw it, I began to feel better. It read:

CHATEAU BOW-WOW
A Special Boarding House
For Special Cats and Dogs

"Look, Chester," I said to the box sitting beside me, "there's a sign on the gate over there. You know what it says?"

"I give up," Chester replied. " 'Abandon All Hope Ye Who Enter Here'?"

I squinted my eyes to see if I could make out any fine print. "No," I answered after looking carefully, "but it says we're special."

"Hmmph," Chester grunted.

"And here's something you'll appreciate," I added, hoping this might cheer him up a little, "it also says 'cats and dogs.' You see, this place is for cats, too. And the sign even puts cats first. Isn't that nice, Chester?"

Chester raised his head to window-level and looked out at the sign. He didn't change his grumpy expression a bit as he said to me, "They probably did it alphabetically." And he dropped out of sight again.

Just then the front door of the office opened and Toby came running out. "Here they are," he called to the strange-looking chap who loped along slowly behind him. This fellow, whoever he was, was older than Toby and Pete but not as old as Mr. and Mrs. Monroe. Having seen some of Mr. Monroe's college students when they'd come to the house to beg for mercy, I estimated that this new chap was roughly their age. He had a shag of brown hair that kept falling into his eyes and a T-shirt that spilled out over the top of his pants. His sneakers were untied, and as he was coming toward us, he stepped on one of the laces and almost fell on his face.

Toby opened Chester's carrier and pulled the reluctant cat out. Chester hung from Toby's arms like Spanish moss and wore an expression that would have soured milk chocolate.

"This is Chester," Toby said, by way of introduction. "Chester, this is Harrison."

Chester turned to me with a smirk. "What am I supposed to do now?" he asked. "Curtsy?"

Harrison, I thought. What a weird name for a person.

"Hey there, kitty," Harrison said, instantly not endearing himself to Chester.

"And this," Toby went on, "is Harold."

"Wow," Harrison said. "What a weird name for a dog."

I looked at Harrison. Harrison looked at me. I thought to myself, this Harrison fellow really has a knack for putting the wrong foot forward.

"Well," Harrison said, "you guys are the last of the arrivals for this week. Now we've got a full house."

The door to the office popped open, and a girl with red hair and a lot of freckles stuck her head out. She seemed to be about the same age as Harrison, but she looked more tucked in.

"Harrison," she called, "do you know where Chester's file is? Dr. Greenbriar wants to look at it while the Monroes are here, and I can't find it anywhere."

"But you were looking at it this morning, Jill," Harrison answered.

"I know, I know," the girl named Jill said, shaking her head. "I just can't remember where I put it. I was hoping you'd seen it."

Harrison shrugged his shoulders and smiled at Jill. "Wish I could help you out," he said, "but I don't pay much attention to the files. That's your territory."

Jill sighed. "I don't know what's the matter with me lately. I'm so tired from all this work I can't remember where I put anything anymore."

"I guess old age is setting in," Harrison said with a laugh.

"Ha ha," Jill answered without one. And she went back inside, letting the door slam behind her.

Chester gave me a look that said he was clearly unimpressed with the staff.

The door opened a third time, and Dr. Greenbriar stepped outside with the rest of the Monroes. I became nervous at once. There's nothing like the sight of a white jacket with creepy little stains all over the front of it to get the old heart pumping.

Dr. Greenbriar walked in our direction, his movements steady and unwavering. The light reflected strangely off his glasses so that it was hard to see what was going on under his thick, bushy eyebrows. When he spoke, his words came as slowly and evenly as his steps.

"Hello, Chester. Hello, Harold," he said to us both as if he were not sure which of us was which.

Chester was apparently as delighted to see Dr. Greenbriar as I was, since his response to the doctor's hello was to begin hissing and shedding hair frantically all over Toby. Dr. Greenbriar just smiled.

"Now, now, Chester, what's the matter, hmmm? You're not afraid, are you?" I suppose his words should have been comforting, but I could feel myself beginning to shake. "You're both going to have a *won*derful time here at Chateau Bow-Wow while your family is away. Aren't they, Harrison?" Harrison looked at Dr. Greenbriar as if he were crazy. The doctor turned back to us. "Harrison and Jill are going to take good care of you. There's nothing to worry about."

Mrs. Monroe seemed a little uneasy. "Are you sure everything will be all right, doctor?" she asked. "I don't mean to question you, but—"

"Everything will be just *fine,* Mrs. Monroe," he answered her sharply. "Surely you don't question my staff?"

Mrs. Monroe's eyes grew wide. "N . . . no, of course not," she answered, taken aback.

"Harrison has worked for me for three summers now, and Jill is studying to be a veterinarian. I trust them both completely. As should you."

"But we thought you'd—" Mr. Monroe started to speak, but was cut off by the doctor.

"Yes, yes, I know. But I simply must take some time off. No one appreciates just how hard I work." His face took on a pained expression as he continued. "This has been a difficult summer. I'll work myself into a collapse if I don't get away." With furrowed brow, he looked into Mrs. Monroe's eyes. Then his features relaxed. "Anyway," he went on, "it isn't as if I were going to the other side of the world. I'll be right here in town, just a phone call away, should any problems come up. I know you have two very special pets here, and believe me, nothing is going to happen to them."

Harrison snorted. *"This* is a special pet?" he asked, pointing to Chester. Chester, who had calmed down a bit, began hissing at Harrison.

"Oh yes," Dr. Greenbriar replied seriously, "Chester is a very special cat. Most . . . *unusual.* Isn't that so, Mr. and Mrs. Monroe?"

"Unusual, hmmm," Mr. Monroe said, reflecting, "I'd say that's *just* the word for Chester. Wouldn't you, dear?"

"That's the word all right," Mrs. Monroe agreed.

At that moment, Jill came through the gate marked "Chateau Bow-Bow." She tripped on a tree stump as she moved toward us. Chester dropped his head sadly. I heard him sigh, I assumed in resignation to his fate.

"Okay, their bungalows are all ready," she said as she approached. She took Chester from Toby and carried him off. He didn't even resist as they disappeared into the world beyond the gate.

"Bungalows are what we call cages here at Chateau Bow-Wow," Dr. Greenbriar was saying to the Monroes. "We think it has more class."

"Oh yes," Mrs. Monroe answered. "Class. Yes." She and Mr. Monroe exchanged a look.

"Well, we should be going," Mr. Monroe said then. "Come on, boys, let's leave Harold to his new home."

Suddenly, Toby threw himself around my neck.

"Goodbye, Harold," he cried. "I'm going to miss you. Be a good dog, okay?" I felt a tear come to my eye.

Pete snickered. "Yeah, Harold," he said sarcastically, "try not to stink up the joint." I felt a bite coming to my teeth.

"Bye, Harold," Mr. Monroe said, leaning down to pat me on the head. "Remember," he added in a whisper, "it's good for the soul."

"Harold," Mrs. Monroe said firmly, "be of good cheer. And keep your eye on Chester, will you? Try to keep him out of trouble." Mrs. Monroe often left me with instructions, but rarely so impossible a task as this. Still, I vowed inside myself to do my best.

Toby was holding me tightly. His tears flowed freely now. "I don't want to leave Harold, Mom," he was saying between sniffs. A lump formed in my throat.

Gently, Mrs. Monroe separated Toby from my neck. As she led him by the hand to the car, Harrison took me by the collar to the waiting gate. Just as I was about to enter, I looked back at Toby who was waving to me sadly. A tear at last escaped my eye, and I turned to step through the gate.

Harrison pulled the door shut, and Chester's words popped into my head. "Abandon all hope," he had said, "ye who enter here."

ONCE inside the gate, I got my first real look at my new home, as Mr. Monroe had called it. Chateau Bow-Wow consisted of nine bungalows. (Whatever they were called, they looked like cages to me.) These stood on three sides of a big grassy play area, which Harrison referred to as the compound. The fourth side of the compound was the back wall of the house. A door in this wall led directly into Dr. Greenbriar's office. This door and the main gate seemed to be the only ways to get in or out of the place. A high wooden fence stood behind all the bungalows. It was impossible to see over it, and the only relief from the drabness within was the presence of a few trees here and there.

Oh well, I thought, I had been right about one thing. The Waldorf-Astoria it wasn't.

Harrison led me to the first bungalow we came to after entering the compound. I was relieved to see that Chester was being housed next door. After Harrison left me, I whispered to Chester through the wall.

"What's it like where you are?" I asked. "This isn't so bad. I've got a nice carpet on the floor and a couple of rubber bones for chewing. It's not home, but at least they've tried to give it a personal touch."

"Oh really?" Chester snapped back. "Like what? Aside from a disgusting looking lump of cloth hanging from a string in here, there isn't much in the way of interior decoration."

"Oh, I'm sorry to hear that, Chester."

"It looks as if it's been hanging here since they built the place," he went on. "Probably supposed to be some sort of cat plaything. To tell you the truth, it looks like a mouse with a serious medical condition."

"I'm sorry," I said again.

"Probably got that way from eating the food here," he muttered.

"Oh, this is nice," I said, noticing my food dish for the first time. "It says 'Doggie's Din-Din' on the side. Does your dinner bowl say anything?"

There was a long silence from the other side of the wall.

"Chester? Chester?"

"I hear you, Harold."

"Does your food dish say anything?"

"Yes, Harold. It says, 'Tuna Tonite! Kitty's Delite!' "

"Oh, that's cute, Chester. Don't you think so?"

"I may throw up."

"Pardon?"

"Never mind, Harold."

After a pause, Chester spoke again.

"Harold?"

"Yes, Chester?"

"This place is a loony bin, Harold. Any place that has a dead mouse hanging on a string as guest room decor is a loony bin."

"Oh, Chester, I think you're exaggerating—" I started to say, but I was cut off by a sudden burst of barking from the two dogs in the bungalows directly across from ours. Straight ahead of me was a bulldog in a white turtleneck sweater. Next to him was a French poodle. They seemed to be in the middle of an argument, and it was the poodle who spoke first.

"Oh, yes, yes!" she was saying. "Over and over you say the same thing. But don't think I am so easily fooled, Monsieur Max. You cannot pull the —how you say—wool over these eyes so easily."

"Louise, lower your voice," the bulldog replied. "Everyone can hear you."

"Let them! I do not care! Why should I? After what you've done to me? Humph!"

Even at a distance, I could see that Max was embarrassed. He tried to pull his head further back into the turtleneck sweater, which already threatened to engulf him. He kept pacing back and forth as they spoke.

"So?" Louise pressed on relentlessly. "What do you have to say for yourself, Monsieur Fancy-Pants?"

"I think you're making a mountain out of a molehill, that's what I have to say," Max responded. "You're making a little hello into—"

"A little hello?!?" Louise shot back. "This kind of little hello, as you call it, I will make into a big *au revoir*—that's what I will do with this little hello."

"Louise," a soft breathy voice interjected. I strained my head to see where it was coming from. The speaker was in a bungalow off to my right, but I couldn't see inside.

"Oh no!" Louise exploded. "This is too—oh, what is that word!? Oh yes—much. Now *she* wants to speak!"

"Now, Louise," Max said, his anger building, "she has just as much right to speak as you do."

"Yes, yes, defend her, why don't you?"

"Louise, I don't need defendin'," said the feathery voice. I noticed the speaker had a slight Southern accent. "I've done nothin' wrong."

"Max is mine! Do you hear me, Scarlett?" Louise fairly ranted across the empty space.

"Georgette," the voice responded gently.

"What?" Louise shrieked.

"My name is Georgette," Georgette repeated.

"Scarlett, Georgette—it's all the same to me. You may want him, but he's mine, do you hear? Mine!"

"Louise!" Max bellowed in a full, rich voice. "Enough! I've had enough of your wild accusations! Now, let it be!"

There was the sound of a crash, and Louise vanished to the back of her bungalow. Max looked sullenly out into the distance.

"Oh dear," Chester said drily next door, "I do believe Louise has thrown her din-din dish against the wall." And then he let out a screech.

"What is it, Chester?" I cried. "What's wrong?"

"Something—something—landed on my door. I don't know . . . what . . . what . . ."

"You've got to help me!" a new voice hissed eerily. There was the sound of wire rattling. "I can't take it anymore."

"Chester, is that you?" I whispered. "Is this some kind of joke?" Suddenly, a head appeared upside-down over the edge of my bungalow. I jumped and hit my own head on the ceiling. That must have jarred my visitor, for he flopped to the ground before my door.

"You're new here, aren't you, buster?" he snarled.

"Uh, yes, yes, I am," I replied, trying to size up the vision before me. He was a cat, that much was clear, but a cat unlike any I'd ever seen. He looked like a walking, talking, patchwork quilt.

He glanced furtively over his shoulder before he spoke again, and then it was in a low, intense whisper. "Tuesday," he uttered. "Over the wall. Don't tell the others. Just you and me."

"Just you and me," I repeated. I didn't have a clue as to what he was talking about.

"Sshh," he said quickly, "not so loud. We'll get out of here, pal, don't worry about it."

"Oh, I'm not," I answered. "At least, I think I'm not."

"Okay, just keep cool." Again, he looked around him. "Watch out!" he snapped all at once. "It's them!" And he was gone.

I cast my eyes in the direction he'd just been looking and saw Harrison and Jill coming with our dinners.

"Oh no," Jill was saying, "will you look at that? Lyle's gotten out again. He's a regular terror. Come on, Lyle, let's go now. Come on, be a nice kitty."

Lyle swept by my bungalow, flattening himself against it as if trying to escape a searchlight. I could see he was the very same cat who had just been talking with me. Harrison swooped down on him suddenly and had him back in his bungalow a few seconds later. I heard Lyle muttering under his breath all the way.

"You know," Jill said to Harrison as he returned to passing out our dinners, "we're going to have to do something about that cat. He gets out of his cage all the—"

"Bungalow," Harrison mumbled irritably.

"Right," she said, "I stand corrected. Oh, by the way, I found Chester's file. It was under your stack of comic books."

"Oh?" Harrison looked up from Max's bungalow, a puzzled look on his face. "I wonder how it got there."

"That's what I wondered," Jill said. "Why do you read those things anyway?"

"Comic books?" Harrison shrugged. "It's something to do," he said simply.

Jill stopped where she was and regarded Harrison. Shaking her head, she said. "What are you going to do, Harrison? Read comic books all your life? Don't you want to *be* something?"

"You mean, go to college like you?" he asked. "No thanks. I don't have the time. I want to retire at twenty-one. All I have to do first is make a million bucks."

"Oh, is that all?" Jill replied. "And how will you do that, if I may ask?"

"*That* is what I haven't figured out yet. But don't worry. I will. I'm thinking all the time."

"I'll bet you are," Jill said. "I'll just bet you are."

"Oh, I am." There was a growl of thunder. "We'd better hurry," Harrison said. "It may start raining."

Quickly, they finished dishing out our food and started toward the door. Jill turned back. "Okay, everyone," she called out, "enjoy your dinners! I'll check in on you later."

I stared down at the fare that had been set before me and wondered what Chester had been so worried about. After all, any place that would put a sprig of parsley on top of a bowl of dog food couldn't be all bad. Mold and rainwater, indeed! I dug in.

IT WAS much later that night when we first heard it. Jill had already checked in on us as promised, and now the sounds of snoring and deep breathing convinced me that most of the guests at Chateau Bow-Wow were already fast asleep.

I was thinking what a strange bunch they were: Max, Louise, Georgette, Lyle—Dr. Greenbriar and Harrison and Jill. Who would I meet tomorrow? I wondered. I was just about to ask Chester what he thought, when—

"*Aaah-ooooooooooooooo!*"

I sat bolt upright, a violent chill racing down my spine.

"Chester!" I cried. "Did you hear—"

"*Aaah-ooooooooooooooo!*" it went again.

It was a howl, of that I was sure. But a howl so terrible, it was unlike the howl of any dog I'd ever heard. Apparently, Chester felt the same way.

"Werewolves!" I heard him utter from his bungalow next door.

"Oh come on, Chester," I said, "you're letting your imagination run wild."

"Werewolves!" he exclaimed again, as the howls reverberated through the night air, alternating with the thunder, which was growing in loudness and intensity.

"Beware!" Chester hissed at me. "Beware!"

"*Aaaaah-oooooooooooooooooooooo!*" went the cry in the night.

There was a sudden silence. Exhausted, but unable to sleep, we sat, side by side, staring into the blackness before us. I held my breath in anticipation of the next sound I would hear. As it turned out, it was Chester.

"Chateau Bow-Wow, my foot," he uttered in a deep, throaty voice. "Welcome to Howliday Inn."

THREE

An Uneasy Calm

I AWAKENED to the sound of rain pelting the roof above me. As my eyes began to focus, I found myself staring at the words, "A Bow-*Wow* Breakfast." After a moment of confusion, I realized I was reading the side of my new food dish. What I saw when I raised my head a little was not what I personally would have described as a bow-wow anything. My dish was heaped with some sort of grayish gruel that was rivaled in dreariness only by the day outside. Perhaps Chester had been right, after all.

"Chester," I called out over the patter of the falling rain. "Chester, are you there?"

"Of course I'm here," he answered churlishly.

"Where'd you think I'd be on a day like this? Out on the golf course perfecting my putt?"

"How did you sleep?" I asked, ignoring his early morning grumpiness. By this time in our lives together, I was used to it.

"Oh, fine. Fine. Why should I let the incessant howling of werewolves disturb my slumber?"

I didn't take up the issue of werewolves with Chester just then, because I'd finished eating my breakfast and discovered the words "Have a Nice Day!" at the bottom of my dish.

"Chester, does your food dish——"

"If you're going to ask me to discuss the attack of cutes this place is suffering from, I refuse," Chester grumbled. "If I wanted my fortune told every time I ate, I could have gone to a Chinese restaurant." And with that, he let out a great sigh and went back to sleep.

I could tell that any attempts at further conversation would prove futile, so I fell back asleep, too, waiting for something else to happen and wishing I were back home.

* * *

BY THE TIME I woke again, the rain had stopped and the something else I'd been waiting for was about to happen. Harrison and Jill were going from bungalow to bungalow opening the doors.

"Okay, animals, let's go," Harrison was saying in a bored sort of way. "Exercise time."

"Thank goodness it stopped raining," Jill called out. "I thought I'd go crazy if I had to spend another minute working on those charts."

"There's still the office to clean," Harrison said, "and the storage shed."

"Harrison," Jill replied, "we don't have to do it *all* today."

"Oh yes, we do," Harrison answered with some urgency.

Jill put her hands on her hips and looked at Harrison with wonder. "You're really something, you know that, Harrison?"

"Am I? Gee, thanks."

"I didn't mean it as a compliment."

"Oh."

"I mean you blow hot and cold. Like yesterday, all you wanted to do was lie around and read your

comic books all day. Today, you can't stop working, and you're driving me crazy. What's with you,
anyway?"

"Who knows?" Harrison replied. "Maybe I'm
getting ambitious. You'd like that, wouldn't you?"
He smiled in Jill's direction, revealing the rem-
nants of that morning's breakfast neatly lodged
between his two front teeth.

In disgust, Jill turned away and poked her head
inside my door. "Good morning, Harold," she
murmured softly. "I hope you had a good sleep
your first night at Chateau Bow-Wow." I allowed
myself to be coaxed out into the muddy outdoors.
I wasn't too thrilled with the condition of the
ground, but was happy just to have the chance to
stretch my legs and move about.

"Where is that storage shed, anyway?" Jill
asked after a moment, continuing her conversation with Harrison as she unlocked Chester's door.

"Out back," Harrison answered, pointing to the
far corner of the compound. "Right outside the
fence near Howard's bungalow."

"Oh."

"But there's no entrance from here. You have to go around the outside wall," Harrison went on. "That's why it's such a pain to clean."

Jill groaned. "That's too bad," she said, picking Chester up and stroking him. Chester's face looked like a car accident. Obviously, he had not slept well at all. "Well, I guess we'd better get to it." She put Chester down and headed for the gate.

"Aren't you forgetting something?" Harrison asked.

Jill looked blankly around her, then quizzically at Harrison.

"Lyle," Harrison said simply. "You didn't let Lyle out of his bungalow."

Jill shook her head slowly. "Oh, of course," she said at last, "I guess I'm just so used to Lyle getting out all by himself, it doesn't even occur to me to unlock his door anymore." I watched as she opened Lyle's door and then walked to the gate, tripping over a small rock that was in her path.

Watching her, Chester dropped his head and moaned.

"All right, everybody," Harrison called out,

"hurry up and enjoy yourselves before it starts raining again." And then he too went out the front gate, carefully locking it after him.

Chester and I looked back to discover Max bounding spiritedly in our direction. With his natty turtleneck sweater and his square shoulders and jaw, he resembled the captain of a college football team.

I remarked on my observation to Chester, whose only response was a rather anemic, "Yea team. Rah. Rah. Rah." Then, he added, "If he says anything athletic, I'll scream."

Max stopped abruptly before us.

"Want to jog?" he blurted out.

True to his word, Chester let out a bloodcurdling screech and immediately turned on his heels. Max appeared to take it in stride.

"I'm Max," he said.

"I'm Harold," I replied politely. "And this is— uh, that was—Chester," I added, introducing Max to Chester's retreating hindside.

"Pleased to meet you both," Max said with a nod to Chester's tail. He returned his gaze to me.

"So, Harold, you want to jog?"

I remembered the one time I'd tried jogging with Pete and Mr. Monroe and had had to be carried home on the back of Pete's bike.

"Uh . . . well, no . . . uh, not really . . . uh . . ." I stated emphatically.

"Helps work out your aggressions," Max countered.

"I don't have any aggressions," I said honestly.

Max seemed disappointed. "So you don't jog, eh?" he asked a little sadly.

"No," I told him again, disappointed that he was disappointed.

"Well, then, now's the time to start. Come on." I could see that Max was not going to be a pushover. I, on the other hand, was and always have been a pushover, so before I could say anything more I found myself trotting, somewhat breathlessly, alongside Max.

"The thing is," Max said after a moment, "you have to get your exercise when you can around here. They only let us out for a few hours in the afternoon. Of course . . ." and he looked around him before he continued, ". . . it's easy to unlock the doors from the inside. Anybody can do it, Harold. Even you."

"Oh, thanks," I said. Or at least, I think that's what I said. I was having a little trouble getting my words out and breathing at the same time. In a burst, I asked, "Do the others know?"

"About getting out? Oh, sure. Everyone knows how to do it. I'll show you later. Lyle's the only one dumb enough to do it when Harrison and Jill are around. The rest of us wait until after supper, when they've gone home."

Suddenly, Max called out, "Taxi! Taxi!" I thought he'd completely flipped.

"Uh, Max," I said, "I'm not sure how to tell you this, but I don't think there's a cab for miles of this place. Besides," I went on between wheezes, "if you're getting tired . . . we don't . . . have to . . . ride. We could . . . just stop . . . running."

"You don't understand," Max said, without once stopping to catch his breath, "I'm not calling a taxi. I'm calling Taxi." He nodded to my right, and I glanced over to see one of the oddest-looking dogs I'd ever encountered, waddling frantically in our direction.

"What kind of dog is this?" I asked.

"Who knows?" Max replied. "I don't think poor Taxi himself knows for sure. He's one part of everything, I guess. He's a good mutt, though. A little on the slow side, if you get my drift, and he tends to be something of a clinging vine, but—"

"What do you mean?" I asked.

"I don't know what it is, but some days he sticks to me like glue. Seems to think the sun rises and sets on me," Max said, without apparent displeasure.

Taxi joined us then, falling into step beside Max. He regarded Max with a look that was one degree away from idol worship. I could see what Max had meant.

"Hi, Max," he said.

"Hey, Taxi, how're you doin'?" Max replied gruffly. "Taxi, I want you to meet Harold."

Taxi nodded absently in my direction. "How are

you feeling today, Max?" he asked.

"Not bad. Not bad. Taxi, I said I want you to meet Harold."

Once again, Taxi nodded his head in a vague sort of way, not really acknowledging my presence. Of course, at that moment I was wondering how much longer it would be before my presence became my past. I could barely catch my breath, and my tongue was hanging somewhere around my knees.

"Had enough?" asked Max, brimming with energy.

". . . uh . . . uh . . . uh . . . uh . . ."

"I guess you have. Come on, let's head for the cooler and take a break."

At the community water cooler, my breathing returned to normal and Taxi noticed me at last.

"Oh, hello," he said as if seeing me for the first time, "who are you?"

"I'm Harold," I replied.

"Harold, Harold," he said, a puzzled look on his face. "Where have I heard that name before?"

"I just introduced you," Max said.

"Oh."

I looked at Taxi. Max was right. He really was on the slow side.

"Are you okay, Max? You're really feeling all right?" Taxi asked.

"Sure, sure," Max snapped, a little irritably. "Why do you keep asking?"

"Well, after that fight last night . . . I mean . . ."

"Oh, *that*," Max answered.

Taxi and I looked at Max as his face grew red beneath his hair. When he returned our gaze, he looked a little embarrassed and not just a little angry.

"Acchh, women!" he uttered. "What a nuisance they are sometimes. That Louise can be so unreasonable."

I glanced over at Louise's bungalow and saw that she was watching us. I felt a little sorry for her.

Max went on. "Just because Georgette and I have said hello a few times, she thinks we're going to run off together." He looked about him and

then in a low voice added, "As if we could get out of here even if we wanted to."

Taxi nodded his head in sympathy. He looked up at Max with wide eyes and sighed deeply. "It must be pretty hard sometimes," he said.

"Yup," Max grunted. "Women. Sometimes I think I'd be better off without them."

There was a moment of silence. All at once, Taxi's face lit up. "Oh, Max," he said excitedly, "you just reminded me of this television show I saw last week. The man said just what you did."

"What's that?" Max asked.

" 'Women. Sometimes I think I'd be better off without them,' " Taxi repeated.

"And then what did he say?" Max asked.

"Nothing. He murdered his wife."

I looked at Taxi. He looked at Max. Max stared straight ahead in the direction of Louise's bungalow.

"That's terrible," he said softly.

Taxi just shrugged his shoulders and began drinking again. He looked up after a moment, water dripping from his lips, and said, "I don't think so."

I looked at him in surprise. "How can you say such an awful thing?" I asked.

"Oh, I wouldn't!" Taxi said.

"But you just did."

"Did what?"

"Say such a thing."

"Did I?"

I was getting confused. "Yes, of course you did. You just said it wasn't such a terrible thing for a man to murder his wife."

"Oh," Taxi said, thinking it over. "Well, I guess I must have meant it then." I could see that holding a conversation with Taxi was definitely going to be a challenge.

"She wasn't a very nice person," Taxi added, as if that made everything okay.

"Still, that's no reason—" I started to say when Max cut me off.

"How'd he do it?" he asked suddenly, turning his gaze from Louise's bungalow to Taxi.

"Poison," Taxi answered simply. And then: "In her soup."

"Hmmm," was Max's only reply.

I observed him for a moment. He must have noticed me, for he laughed suddenly and said, "Well, that's one way of handling women, I suppose."

"I suppose," I replied, not at all sure I liked being part of this conversation.

"Yes," Max went on thoughtfully. "Murder is one way. Murder in its infinite varieties. Poison, stabbing, drowning, strangling—"

"Split pea," Taxi interjected.

Max and I looked at him. "He put poison in her split pea soup," he explained.

"Oh," I said.

"Ah," said Max.

"Yoo-hoo," called a new voice.

We all turned and saw a tiny white French poodle standing a few feet away.

"Georgette," Max whispered.

"Good afternoon, Max," Georgette cooed as she approached the water cooler. She smelled of honeysuckle and magnolias. She also smelled of trouble. "How're you doin' after that terrible fight? I just felt so awful-awful bad about it, I couldn't sleep a wink all night worryin' about you." And here she yawned, showing us, I gathered, how much she had suffered on Max's account.

"Don't believe a word of it," Taxi whispered to me.

Max started pawing the ground self-consciously. "Aw, shucks," he said at last. "I'm fine today. Thanks for asking."

"Oh, that's silly," Georgette replied.

"What is?" Max asked, grinning openly now.

"Thankin' me for carin' about you," Georgette answered.

"Aw, shucks," Max said again. It struck me that when Georgette came around, Max's vocabulary suffered.

It was then I noticed that Louise had joined us.

"Hah!" she exclaimed. " 'Aw, shucks,' says Monsieur Max. I come over here to tell you that I am—how you say—sorry that we have had our little fight. And what do I hear? 'Aw, shucks!' Well, *mon ami,* is this what you will say when I am no longer around? Eh? 'Aw, shucks'? Because if you are keeping this up much longer with Hester Prynne here—"

"Georgette," Georgette said softly.

"Georgette, Hester, what am I caring? If you think you can have your Louise and your Mademoiselle Aw-Shucks, too, you are sadly mis-shapen!" I think she meant to say "mistaken" but she was so overwrought at this point, it was un-derstandable that the word came out wrong. I wanted to console her, but she left us with a grand flourish before anyone, including Max, could speak. Just as she was about to reach her bunga-low, Lyle suddenly pounced on her back.

"Bombs away!" he cried.

Louise screamed. "What are you doing?! You are a very crazy cat, you nutty Lyle, you! Get off me this instant!"

Lyle didn't seem to be paying any attention to Louise's screams. In fact, it appeared that he was talking to someone else entirely.

"Ace-One to Four-Seven. Come in, Four-Seven. Have bombed the target area. Meeting resistance. Roger. Over and out."

Max ran over to Louise to help. "Lyle!" he commanded. "Stop this at once!"

"Don't you be helping me!" Louise cried. "I will take care of myself, *merci*-you-very-much." Max backed off, tucking himself as far into his sweater as possible.

Louise turned her head around so that she was staring directly into Lyle's eyes.

Lyle mumbled under his breath as if talking into a headset. "Enemy contact. Enemy contact. Standby. Mayday! Mayday!"

"Now you listen to me," Louise said in a low, threatening tone. Lyle's eyes went wild, and he stopped talking immediately. "We know all about you here. Do not think we are playing the fools. You have been driving us all—what is it?—ah, yes, pineapples . . ."

"I think she means bananas," Georgette whispered across the way to no one in particular.

". . . but I, for one, have had enough. Do you understand me, Monsieur Lyle? Enough pineapples you have driven me! You will not make me into a fruit salad, *n'est-ce pas?* Now, get off my back and do not ever again use me for a landing stripe!"

Lyle hissed at her and jumped off her back. He dashed to the other side of the compound and then he turned suddenly and faced her.

"You haven't seen the end of me, toots!" he shouted. "No one talks to Lyle like that and gets away with it!"

"You are not frightening me, Monsieur Bombs-Away!" Louise yipped back.

There was a sudden crash of thunder, which shook us all. No one spoke for a few seconds; then there came a deep, rumbling sound. I thought at first it was more thunder. Then I realized it was coming from Lyle's direction. I looked at him. He was growling at Louise.

From somewhere deep in his throat, he said, "I don't like being crossed, sister. Just . . . watch . . . out!" He stared at her coolly, and Louise, momentarily stunned, stared back. She looked frightened, and I wondered, for the first time, if indeed there was reason for her to be.

FOUR

The Storm Gathers

ALL AT ONCE Louise broke into a rapid-fire attack of barking. I wanted to check out Max's reaction, but Harrison's voice startled the thought right out of me.

"What's going on in here?" he asked, suddenly entering through the gate. Everyone froze. "What's all this noise? Now calm down, or back into your bungalows you go."

Jill appeared next to him, carrying a large bag of garbage. She was panting slightly. "What was it?" she asked.

"Oh, nothing. Just a dog fight, I guess," Harrison said. Dog fight, I thought, what a quaint expression. I wondered if people ever had dog fights.

As Harrison and Jill turned to go, Jill tripped on the very rock I'd seen her trip over before. The bag of garbage flew out of her hands, spilling its contents all over the ground.

Harrison jumped back as some of the debris landed on his shoe. "What a clumsy oaf!" he shouted. "Can't you do anything right?"

Jill's face turned red. I could see tears coming to her eyes as she spoke. "Well, aren't you Mister Perfect all of a sudden?" she asked, her voice quivering. "If you weren't pushing me so hard, I wouldn't be like this in the first place."

"Maybe if you weren't like this in the first place," Harrison retorted, "you wouldn't think I was pushing you so hard."

Jill's mouth fell open. After a moment, she spoke. "And *maybe* you'd like to work by yourself the rest of the day!"

"Okay, okay," Harrison replied in a softer voice. "I'm sorry. Come on, let's forget it and clean this up."

Jill, sniffling back her tears, knelt in silence and began shoveling tin cans and bottles back into the plastic bag. "I'm sorry, too," she said quietly. "I'm just tired. It's not your fault."

They finished their task in total silence. We all sat motionless, watching them. I guess people *do* have dog fights, I thought.

Just before they went out the gate, Harrison turned back to us and said, "Now, keep it down in here." And once again we were left to ourselves.

I turned to Max, but saw that he and Georgette had wandered off. Their heads were very close together. Taxi was watching them, too, and seemed to be annoyed. When he noticed me looking at him, he said, "A fine thing!" and walked away in a huff.

Suddenly, I found myself alone. I could feel that a light rain was beginning to fall. And a second crack of thunder announced that the storm was about to break again. Not knowing what else to do, I headed back to my bungalow in the hopes that Chester might be around to talk to.

I guess I was so lost in thought that I never saw them, but when I was almost to my bungalow, I tripped. Looking down, I discovered that what had

crossed my path were two long, low dogs, the likes of which I'd never seen before. As politely as I knew how, I spoke.

"Please forgive me for tripping over you," I said.

"Not at all. Not at all," said one. "Indeed, it was our fault for—"

"Yes, yes," said the other. "For walking in your way."

"We weren't watching—" said the first.

"—where we were going," concluded the second.

There was a moment's silence as I looked them over. They were almost identical, and though one had a slightly higher-pitched voice than the other, they spoke as if one mind were encased in two bodies. Their heads did not stop bobbing up and down.

"I'm Harold," I said.

"Howard . . ." said the one with the lower-pitched voice. He nodded his head once.

". . . and Heather," said the other. And she nodded her head crisply.

"We're out for a stroll," Howard continued, as if he owed me an explanation. "We do like a stroll. Of course, Heather here isn't up to—"

"Now, now, now," Heather said, cutting Howard off. "No need to go into all that, is there?" She smiled vaguely in my direction, and our conversation drew to a halt. The rain began to come down more heavily then. I was more than a little relieved to have a reason to excuse myself.

"Well, it was—" I began.

"Yes, yes, it was," Howard said eagerly. "So sorry we have to run, but—"

"Oh, I understand," I said.

"—but, I'm not feeling myself suddenly," Heather added. "Dear, mightn't we—?"

"Yes, yes, of course," Howard said to her. There was a look of great concern in his eyes.

"Goodbye, Harold," he said, as they turned to leave. "We will talk again, I am sure. Oh, and Harold . . . ?"

"Yes?" I asked.

"Beastly sorry about that noise last night. Frightful, what? But we just can't seem to—"

"—help it, really," Heather finished the sentence for him. "Come, dear."

"Quite," was all that Howard said then, and the two of them strolled off, rather more hurriedly, their heads bobbing like pigeons all the way home.

"CHESTER!" I cried as soon as I saw my friend waiting for me in my bungalow. The rain was really coming down by that time.

Chester sat licking a paw and staring into the distance. As he did not respond immediately to my calling, I concluded that he was once again in a state of advance mellowhood. I waited another moment before I spoke again.

"Guess what?" I asked.

Chester looked at me through half-lowered lids. "Harold, you know I hate it when you do that," he said.

"When I do what?"

"When you say 'Guess what?' " he replied with faint disdain. "How am I supposed to guess what, when I don't even know where you're coming from?"

"Oh, sorry," I answered. There was a pause.

"Harold," he said quietly after a moment.

"What?"

"I think we've established that I'm not going to guess what. So why don't you just tell me what's on your mind, hmm? I have a lot to think about, however, and I don't wish to be distracted by trivia."

"Oh, I don't think this is trivia," I said, though

I couldn't be sure since I didn't know what trivia was. "It has to do with these two strange dogs I just met named Howard and Heather. They said they were sorry about the noise last night. Do you think they were the ones who——"

"Is that all?" Chester said sharply, interrupting me. "I figured that out long ago."

"You figured what out?" I asked. I hadn't figured anything out, except that it was Howard and Heather who had been howling all night.

"That Howard and Heather are werewolves."

I couldn't help myself. I chuckled at the thought of those two little dogs being werewolves. To me, they looked more like sausages with legs, and I told Chester so.

"Dachshunds," he replied.

"Gesundheit."

"I didn't sneeze, Harold."

"Oh, but you said——"

"Dachshunds."

"Gesundheit."

"Harold, put the etiquette on the shelf for a minute and listen to me. Howard and Heather are not sausages. They are a kind of dog called dachshunds. Because of their long hair, I am assuming that they are what is known as wire-haired dachshunds."

"But you said they were werewolves."

"It is my belief," Chester went on (and here he drew out his words to give the impression that what he was saying was of the most crucial importance), "that Howard and Heather are a cross between a wire-haired dachshund and . . . a werewolf." He paused and looked at me to check out the impact of what he was saying. There was none. With a slight tremor in his voice, he added, "A most vile and dangerous combination."

I yawned. I knew Chester well enough to know when to respond and when to yawn. This was definitely a time to yawn.

"You don't believe me, do you?" Chester asked. "Well, it doesn't matter, Harold. This isn't the first time you've chosen to ignore my warnings, and I'm sure it won't be the last. Just let it be said that Howard and Heather are to be watched."

"If you ask me," I replied, "Lyle is the one to watch. Now, *there*'s a basket case."

Chester agreed that Lyle was worthy of observation, for he too had witnessed the scene earlier with Louise. "Indeed," he concluded, "I'd say *all* of the guests in this establishment deserve our careful attention. There is an undercurrent of tension here, Harold." He looked out at the pouring rain and the darkening sky. "An undercurrent that will one day erupt with a sudden and terrible force."

There was a loud explosion of thunder. I jumped.

"The storm gathers," Chester commented drily as I landed.

"What shall we do?" I asked.

"Nothing to do. Nothing to do but wait." He lay down then and closed his eyes. "Meanwhile, I'm going to get some sleep—while I still can."

"Mind if I join you?" I asked, not wanting to be alone.

"Not at all," Chester said, making room for me next to him on the rug. I was thinking how hospitable he was being, when I realized that we were in *my* bungalow.

"Just one favor, Harold."

"What's that, Chester?"

"When you dream?"

"Yes?"

"Try not to smack your lips all the time, will you? It drives me crazy."

So promising, I fell into a deep sleep.

THE NEXT THING I remember was the deafening crash of thunder that awakened us. Chester jumped up and ran to the door.

"It's dark!" he cried.

Max and Taxi were in the center of the compound, barking loudly.

"What's going on?" I called out.

"They're late with dinner," Max responded. He and Taxi began barking again, as Georgette ran out and joined them. I noticed how she cuddled up to Max's side and immediately my heart ached for Louise. Since my attention went rather quickly to my stomach, however, my heart didn't ache for long.

"What do you think has happened?" I asked

Chester. "I can't go without food. Dogs aren't meant to be starved. Cats are different. Cats can live off their own fat, but dogs are——"

"Try living off the fat on your brain," Chester said, cutting me off.

Just then, the door of the office swung open and Jill and Harrison rushed out. Jill was wearing an orange slicker, and Harrison carried an umbrella that quickly turned itself inside out, doing neither him nor our dinners any good. I made a mental note to complain about the service. But later. At the moment, all I cared about was that our food was here at last.

The storm was in full force, the wind lashing the rain against us. Harrison and Jill scurried about quickly, calling to each other across the compound. I couldn't hear everything they said, but I did pick up snatches of conversation.

". . . can't understand how we let this happen," Harrison was saying. "We've never been late before. It's your fault, you know. I told you to keep your eye on the clock."

"My fault?" Jill answered. "You were the one

who insisted that we clean the office after we finished the shed. Push, push, push."

"Okay, Jill," Harrison said, with an exasperated tone in his voice, "give it a rest, huh?"

"Give it a rest, he says," Jill muttered to herself. "He doesn't know the meaning of the word." Then turning her attention to us, she said, "Oh, you poor things, you must be starving. Sorry, sorry," she kept saying to everyone. "Sorry," as she put down the food dishes and scurried us back into our bungalows.

I was so relieved to get my dinner, I hardly noticed that I'd gotten soaked by the storm. I was glad, though, when Jill suddenly showed up at the door of my bungalow with a big white towel in her hands.

"Sorry to have to interrupt you, Harold," she said sweetly, "but let me dry you off a little so you can enjoy the rest of your dinner." Jill's hands felt good as she rubbed me down, and I would have happily rolled over for a complete MTR (that's "massage and tummy rub" to you laymen) had I not been so anxious to return to eating dinner. "I don't know where my head is these days," she said as she rubbed the hair along my back. "I completely forgot about feeding you guys tonight. And then we raced out here so fast, I left the towels inside and let the door slam shut behind me." She laughed to herself and shook her head. "I guess I need a rest, too," she said. "Dr. Greenbriar and I have been working so hard these past few weeks, I'm ready to drop. And Harrison —but I can't blame him," she said seriously. "That's no excuse. It would be awful if something happened just because I let myself get a little tired and careless."

"Jill," Harrison called, "I've finished drying the rest of them. I'm going back in."

"Okay," Jill shouted back above the din of the rain. "I'll be right there."

She turned to me and scratched me behind the ears. "Okay, Harold, that's it. Enjoy your dinner now. And get a good night's sleep. Night-night."

And she was gone.

I liked Jill, I thought, as I plunged back into my food. She was clumsy and forgetful it was true, but she seemed nice enough. As for Harrison, well, I wasn't sure what to make of him. There was something about him that made me nervous. Besides, anybody who preferred reading comic books to chewing on them was a little suspect in my eyes.

Later that night, I tried to sleep. But the raging storm and the determined howling of Howard and Heather kept startling me awake. And then I started thinking about what Chester had said earlier. What were his exact words? Something about an undercurrent of tension that would one day erupt with a terrible force. What could he mean? I wondered.

Little did I imagine then, tossing and turning in my sleep, that the terrible eruption Chester had predicted had already occurred.

FIVE

"She's Gone!"

THE NEXT MORNING, I was startled out of my sleep by the sound of Harrison's voice. "Oh no!" he cried.

I moved quickly to the front of my bungalow to see what was going on. So did everyone else. Harrison stood in the center of the compound, shaking his head, as Jill flew out of the office door.

"What is it?" she shouted. "What's happened?"

Harrison pointed at Louise's bungalow. The door was wide open.

"She's gone!" he proclaimed.

Immediately, I shifted my gaze to Max. Our eyes met. His jaw fell open, as a look of shock and bewilderment swept over him.

"But how?" Jill asked. "This has never happened before, has it?"

"Not in the three summers I've worked here," Harrison replied. Slowly, he surveyed the entire compound, looking at each of us in turn. Then, suddenly, he called out, "Look!"

We all turned our heads sharply in the direction he was pointing. Unfortunately, I hit my nose on the wall of my bungalow and I couldn't see a thing except stars. So it took Jill's words to make clear what it was that had so astonished him.

"Oh no," she said. "The gate! It's open!"

"How can it be?" Harrison asked. "There's no way any of the animals could open that lock."

"I don't know," Jill said, her brow wrinkled in confusion and distress. "Unless one of us . . ." She stopped speaking then, and a strange expression came over her face.

"What is it?" Harrison asked. "What's the matter?"

"I did it," she said after a minute. Her voice was soft and a little wavery.

"What do you mean?" Harrison queried. His eyebrows came together to form a hedge across his forehead.

"I did it," Jill repeated. "I left the gate open. Don't you remember? When I ran in to get the towels, I accidentally let the office door lock behind me, so I had to go back by the gate. I was in such a hurry and it was raining so badly, I guess I just didn't notice . . . I . . ." Her shoulders slumped, and it was another moment before she spoke again. In the interim, a flash of lightning ripped through the sky, letting us know that the storm was not yet over. "Oh, I feel terrible," Jill went on. "It's all my fault. What are we going to do?"

Much to my surprise, Harrison came over to Jill and put his arm around her shoulders. "Don't worry," he said softly, "we'll find her. It was a mistake. It could have happened to anyone. Come on. Let's give everyone breakfast, and then you and I will go out looking for her."

Jill seemed as surprised as I was at Harrison's concern. She looked at him warily out of the corner of her eyes. "What if we don't find her?" she asked.

"Then she'll find us," Harrison said calmly. "She'll wind her way back home sooner or later." He smiled then and said gently, "Okay?"

"Okay," Jill replied, accepting Harrison's attempts at reassurance, and together they went back inside the office.

AFTER breakfast, Chester and I put our heads together to consider Louise's escape. Harrison and Jill had let us out early for exercise, since there was no way of knowing when the storm would start up again.

"What did I tell you?" Chester asked me.

"I give up," I answered, not at all sure what he was referring to.

"Didn't I say there would be trouble?"

"What trouble?" I countered. "Louise ran away. Makes sense, if you ask me."

"Oh, really?"

"Sure."

"Would you care to enlarge on your theory?"

"I'd be delighted," I replied. "Louise was very upset about Max's flirting with Georgette. Agreed?"

"Agreed."

"So, when she saw that the front gate had been left open last night, she seized the opportunity to run off and teach Max a lesson. She'll be back."

"And that's it?"

"Simple, really. Just opened the door to her bungalow, and out she went."

"Mmm-hmm," Chester replied, licking his paws. His long tongue moved slowly between each of his toes as he reflected on what I'd said. No doubt he was impressed with my powers of deduction. "And did she unlock Max's door, too?"

"Huh?" I asked, completely thrown. "What do you mean?"

"What I mean is that Max's door was open this morning, too. You may not have noticed that, but I did. You have to learn to be observant in this business, Harold."

"What business is that, Chester?"

"The business of crime detection," Chester an-

swered, neatly snapping his head in my direction
to look me squarely in the eyes.

"Crime detection?" I responded. I could feel
the hairs along the back of my neck rise slightly.
Chester has always had the ability to alarm me,
often unnecessarily. I was hoping this was the
case. "Chester," I said, "I think you're getting
carried away."

"On the contrary," he replied, "it may well
have been Louise who was carried away."

"Oh," was all I could say, for Max's voice suddenly bellowed throughout Chateau Bow-Wow.

"It's no good," he groaned, "no good!" Chester
and I looked out to see him sitting in the middle
of the compound, a forlorn expression smeared
across his face like after-breakfast jam. The ever-
present Georgette was at his side.

"Now, Max, you mustn't carry on so," she said
softly.

"Hussy," I heard myself utter under my breath.

"I can't help it, Georgette," Max cried, his
voice cracking. "It's all my fault this happened. I
never should have spoken to her the way I did."

I could see Taxi moving in Max's direction; Max looked up and saw him coming.

"I'm sorry, Max, I—" Taxi started to say.

"Not now, Taxi!" Max fairly shouted.

"But, Max—"

"No, Taxi, I want to be alone!" And Max picked himself up and lumbered back to his bungalow. Georgette followed. He turned to her suddenly and said, "Please, Georgette. I need some . . . space."

"Of course," she answered, her feathery voice at its featheriest, "I understand. This is not the time for . . . us."

She turned and walked away, her spirit trailing behind her like a long shadow on a sultry summer day. Taxi, meanwhile, stood in the center of the compound. From the look on his face, he was not pleased that Max had dismissed him so abruptly. After a moment's deliberation, he moved away toward one corner of the compound and began to scratch himself behind the ears.

"Come on," Chester said to me, "we've got some exploring to do."

"Okay," I answered, "but I don't know what you expect to find. Anyway, if you're suspecting Max of anything, I guess you can rule him out now. Boy, is he upset. Poor fella."

"Is he?" Chester asked pointedly. "Perhaps he is a 'poor fella,' as you say. Or perhaps a poor actor putting on a good show."

We were walking in the direction of Louise's bungalow when we bumped into Howard and Heather. They both jumped in surprise.

"Sorry," I said, "I didn't mean to startle you."

"Oh . . . oh . . . it's nothing," Howard said. "No, it's nothing—"

"—at all," said Heather. "Oh my, I'm so jumpy today. I don't feel quite myself. No, I—"

"Sorry about that beastly howling last night, old chap," Howard said to me. He turned with a nod to Chester. "Certainly hope we weren't the cause of Louise's . . . uh . . ."

". . . departure," Heather added. She giggled suddenly. And then, just as suddenly, she gasped and tried to catch her breath.

"What is it?" Howard cried.

"Oh, it's nothing," Heather replied, after letting out a great sigh. "I'm having such trouble breathing today. I don't know what . . . it . . . is . . ." She looked at Howard, her big eyes wide in bewilderment. The two of them stared at each other a long moment, their heads bobbing up and down in unison.

"I think we'd better—" Howard began.

"—go home," Heather finished. "Yes, dear. I think we'd best. Do excuse us," she said, turning to us. "I'm just not—"

"—herself," said Howard. And they turned and left. Chester and I watched them go.

"Typical werewolvian behavior," said Chester, his voice full of authority. I'm sure I would have asked him to elaborate, if it were not for the fact that I didn't really care in the least what he had to say. So I changed the subject.

"Weren't we going to do some exploring?" I asked.

"Yes," Chester answered, snapping himself out of his pensive mood. "Follow me."

I followed Chester to Louise's bungalow, where

we stood for what felt like a long time, staring at the emptiness inside. "Just think," I said, feeling a tear come to my eye," last night she was here. To-day, she's gone."

"Yes," said Chester slowly. "That's exactly the word. 'Gone.' "

"Escaped," I added. "But soon she'll be back with us."

"Nonsense," Chester said scornfully. "She didn't escape. And she won't be back. No one comes back from murder!"

"Murder?"

"Of course, murder," Chester replied evenly. "It's all falling into place, don't you see?"

"What's falling into place?"

"The suspects. The motives. And now the evi-dence," said Chester.

I was confused (which around Chester is a normal state of being, so it didn't alarm me). "What evidence?" I asked.

"Look for yourself," he said, with a nod to-ward the bungalow. "What do you see?"

I surveyed the interior. "A rug. A water dish.

A food dish," I said. "Just like mine."

"Ah, but it isn't just like yours, Harold, and that's the key."

"Why? I don't see anything so different."

"Look again. And this time use your powers of observation, such as they are. *Now,* what do you see?"

I scrunched up my eyes and looked carefully at each square inch of space as if studying for a final exam at obedience school.

"Well?" Chester prodded.

"A rug. A water dish. A food dish," I proclaimed.

Chester sighed and shook his head sadly. "Sometimes I despair, Harold," he uttered. "Allow me to fill you in on what you've missed."

"Please do."

"The rug. How is it different from yours?" I shrugged. "It's all jumbled up," Chester went on. "A real mess, in fact. And the food dish? Almost filled with food. These observations may seem insignificant, but wait, my friend. Now we come to the water dish, perhaps the most significant item of all. And yet it isn't really the water dish, but what lies around it that is so disturbing."

Thoroughly confused, I looked at the water dish and the floor around it. Nothing struck me as unusual.

"But don't you see?" Chester asked. "What is lying all around the water dish?"

"Water?" I ventured.

"Exactly!" he exclaimed triumphantly.

"But what else would you expect to find around a water dish?"

"Ordinarily, the appearance of water around a water dish would not be out of the ordinary in the least. But given the unusual combination of factors, it is most striking. And it will be given serious consideration in our investigation."

Suddenly, Lyle zoomed by us.

"Faster than a speeding bullet—" I heard him call out as he passed. "Able to leap buildings in a single bound!"

Chester shook his head. "That Lyle is a disgrace to the species," he said. Then, back on the track of his previous thought, he said, "Come on, Harold, I need to talk this out with you right now."

We found a quiet spot under a tree in a corner of the compound. The storm seemed to have abated for the moment, and I thought how pleasant it would be just to lie here for a while and commune with nature. But Chester had other ideas.

"The rug, the food dish and the water on the floor all add up to foul play, my dear Harold, don't you see? Signs of a struggle, old boy!" Old boy? I thought. "My guess—and it's only a guess, mind you—is that someone pushed Louise's head into the water while she was drinking. She resisted, which accounts for the spilled water and the wrinkled rug."

"And the food?" I asked.

"She never finished her dinner," Chester said simply. "She was . . . shall we say . . . interrupted."

I must confess Chester's deductions began to awaken in me the possibility that what he was suspecting was true. Still, I wasn't going to give up my theory of Louise's escape so easily.

"What if it happened just as Jill and Harrison

said?" I asked. "Isn't that possible?"

"Sure, it's possible," Chester answered. "But it's unlikely."

"Why?"

"If Louise had run away, it's only logical she would have finished eating her dinner first, since she couldn't have known when she'd be eating her next meal. And why the appearance of a struggle? And why," Chester added, "was Max's door open as well?"

"So you're saying Max did it?"

"I'm not saying anything—yet. Obviously, Max had the motive. And the strength to pull it off. Let us picture the scene: He comes to Louise's bungalow telling her he wants to apologize. She lets him in. He pushes her head into the water. She struggles, but he has the strength to hold her down. Afterward, he drags her body out through the front gate."

"But he's so upset today," I said, still not believing Max capable of such an act.

"Either that or, as I suggested before, he's pretending he is. To throw us off, you see?"

I allowed as how I did. "What about Georgette?" I asked. "She could have done it. I wouldn't put much past her."

"Yes, that's possible, too. The only problem there is that I doubt she has the strength to hold Louise's head down. What's more likely is that they're in cahoots, she and Max. She may have been his accomplice. Unless, of course," and here Chester thought for a moment, "I have the method of the murder itself wrong. Hmm, that will bear some thinking."

In the distance, Lyle dropped from the branch of a tree onto Taxi's head. Taxi, not in the mood to wear Lyle as a hat, shook him off so violently that he landed several feet away. Stunned, he picked himself up and screamed at Taxi, "I can tell when I'm not wanted! Don't think I can't take a hint!" And he stormed off.

"What about Lyle?" I asked. "Do you remember how he threatened Louise yesterday?"

"Indeed, I do," Chester answered, nodding slowly. " 'You haven't seen the end of me,' he said. 'Just watch out!' And you know, Harold,

Lyle is just crazy enough to do it. When you think about it, the murderer could be anyone here."

"Anyone?" I asked, puzzled.

"Anyone!" Chester affirmed. "We know, for instance, that Howard and Heather are part were-wolf—"

"*You* know," I corrected.

"Oh, come on, Harold, no normal dog howls like that."

"That's true," I concurred, "*I* don't."

"True. Of course, you're not normal either, but we'll overlook that for the moment."

"Thank you," I said.

"Besides, werewolves are very hairy. Look at how hairy Howard and Heather are."

"They're wire-haired dachshunds. You said so yourself."

"They're very *hairy* wire-haired dachshunds," Chester countered, refusing to allow logic to blow his theory. "And if they are werewolves, they can change shape anytime they want."

"Huh?" I inquired.

"Werewolves can change into anything, any-

time at all, in order to assist them in their pursuit
of evil." I tried to imagine Howard and Heather
changing shape. It was hard to picture Howard as
a clothes hanger or Heather as a toaster-oven. I
was about to mention this to Chester when he
spoke again.

"You have to admit they were behaving
strangely today," he said. "Guilt, Harold. They
were consumed with guilt!"

I said, "I doubt werewolves feel guilty."

"The guilt comes from the wire-haired dachshund part of them. It's common to the breed."

"Oh," I replied. "And what about Harrison and
Jill? Do you suspect them, too?"

"Of course," said Chester. "They're both a little
on the shady side, if you ask me. Besides, we don't
know the whole story on this Dr. Greenbriar yet.
If you want my opinion, it's more than a little
strange that he's gone off and left us in the care
of these two. I wouldn't be at all surprised if
they're acting on his orders."

"What are you implying?"

"I'm not implying anything," Chester answered

innocently. "I'm just thinking out loud. It's interesting, that's all, that while the doctor is away, Louise disappears. And neither Harrison nor Jill seemed too concerned about letting him know."

"Maybe they want to find Louise first," I suggested.

"Or maybe Greenbriar has ordered them to murder her."

"Oh, Chester," I said. This last was too much. "What about Jill? Didn't you see how upset she was?"

"Again, like Max, it could be she's faking. Or" —and here he paused a moment—"perhaps Harrison is in it alone with the not-so-good doctor. That's a possibility, too."

My head was spinning with Chester's theories. Then I thought of the one suspect he'd left out. "And Taxi?" I asked. "He's too dumb to concoct a murder like this." I didn't like saying it about poor Taxi, but it was true. Chester didn't agree.

"You don't have to be a genius to murder, Harold. No, it isn't Taxi's intelligence that troubles me. It's his strength. He's a timid little fellow.

I can't imagine him holding Louise down long enough to . . ." Here Chester drifted off into thought. Suddenly, his eyes lit up.

"Unless . . ." he said excitedly. "If we change the method of murder . . . then . . ."

"Yes?"

"We know that Taxi is always buttering up to Max, right?"

"Right," I agreed.

"And we know that his feelings were hurt yesterday when Max went off with Georgette instead of spending time with him. We also know he'd do anything to please Max to get back into his good graces."

"But murder?" I asked. I couldn't believe it of Taxi.

"Sure, why not? I was on the wrong track, don't you see? If we believe that Louise was drowned, then Taxi is pretty much ruled out. He wouldn't have the strength. And I doubt that he'd have the guts. But if the method of murder were less direct—if, for instance . . ." and he paused dramatically, ". . . Louise were poisoned—"

I felt a jolt go through me. "Chester!" I cried. "What is it?"

"I just remembered something Taxi said yesterday. Max had just gotten through telling us how sometimes he thought he'd be better off without women."

"Yes?"

"And Taxi told us about a television program he'd seen where a man, feeling the same way, murdered his wife."

"And the method, Harold? What method did he use?"

"Poison."

Chester and I sat very still for a moment. My gaze drifted to where I had seen Taxi sitting a few moments before. He was no longer there.

Could it be? I asked myself. Could Taxi have murdered Louise to please Max? What kind of warped mind existed within that peculiar little body of his?

I turned my head then and, much to my surprise, saw that Taxi was sitting a few feet away. He stared at me in such a cold way that I knew he'd heard every word Chester and I had said about him.

"Taxi!" I said, startled.

He didn't respond, but continued to glare at me.

I swallowed hard and tried to speak again. "I . . . I'm . . ."

Taxi cut me off with a menacing growl, and before I could get another word past my lips, he turned and walked away.

"He heard . . ." I said then to Chester.

"Yes," was all Chester said in reply. But there was something in the way he said it that sent a shiver down my spine.

SIX

The Cat Who Knew Too Much

WITHOUT warning, the sky opened and the rain came down. Lyle and Taxi ran for the shelter of their bungalows. Georgette ran to Max's, and he made no sign for her to leave. Interesting, I thought. Even more interesting was the fact that I was sitting in the middle of a pouring rain watching everyone else run for cover.

"Come on, Chester," I called out, "let's go."

"Don't be ridiculous," he shouted back. "Now is the perfect time for us to investigate."

"Perfect time?" I asked. "Investigate? Are you crazy? It's pouring."

"I know, I know. But Max and Georgette are together, and if we're clever about it, we can eavesdrop on them without their noticing. Follow me." I didn't budge. I couldn't believe Chester wanted to play detective in the middle of a storm. I was all set to return to my bungalow, but the next words he spoke got me.

"If not for me," he said, "do it for Louise."

As we approached Max's bungalow, Chester stopped and beckoned for me to bend down. He whispered, "If we could get up on the roof, we could lean over and hear everything. Give me a boost."

"How am I supposed to do that?" I asked. But Chester had already jumped up on my shoulders and from there to the top of the bungalow. "Oh," I said in answer to my own question. Seeing that I had no one's shoulders to assist me, I had little choice but to take a running leap.

"Softly!" Chester commanded as I landed next to him with a crash. "Nice move," he commented.

"I'm not as quiet as you are, Chester," I said. "I can't help it. I'm big."

"And clumsy! Well, never mind. If they heard us, I'll just go 'Ho! Ho! Ho!' and tell them Christmas is early this year."

We hung over the front of the bungalow, listening as best we could. The rain was coming down even harder now, making it almost impossible to hear what was being said inside. We couldn't see anything either because the door was just a little lower than either of us could reach with our heads.

"Listen," Chester said in a low voice, "I've got to get closer. If you hold me with your front legs, I'll be able to hang down to the top of the door and hear and see what's going on inside."

Well, I wasn't sure this was such a good idea, but as you may have figured out for yourself by now, once Chester has a notion in his head, there's no arguing him out of it. I held onto his back legs with my paws and lowered him to the front door. His tail brushed against my nose. It tickled.

"Chester," I whispered as loudly as I could, "move your tail."

"What?" he whispered back.

"Move your tail. It's tickling my nose."

"I can't hear you, Harold. Now be quiet. I think I can make out what they're saying in there. Lower me a little more."

I pushed myself forward an inch or two in order to lower Chester. With the rain coming down the way it was, the roof was getting pretty slippery and I didn't dare go much further.

"How's that?" I called out.

Chester couldn't hear me, so he didn't answer. Apparently it had worked though because I could see that his ears were standing up sharply, a good sign that he was able to hear something. Whatever he was hearing must have been good because his tail started twitching like crazy. Unfortunately, it was twitching like crazy all over my nose.

"Stop it!" I cried, as the tears started rolling down my face. Boy, did that tickle. "Chester! Chester!" I called out. But by now the rain was really coming down, and he couldn't hear a word I said. No matter which way I turned my head, Chester's tail found my nose. "Chester, you're making me laugh," I cried out desperately. I could feel myself starting to slip off the roof.

Finally, I couldn't stand it any longer. Without realizing what I was doing, I let go of Chester's legs and grabbed his tail. He plunged downward, pulling me with him. Off the slippery roof I tumbled, holding Chester tightly by the tail. Together we landed in a jumble right in front of the door to the bungalow. Max and Georgette turned to discover us lying in a puddle at their doorstep.

"Look, Max," Georgette said, "it's rainin' cats and dogs." She seemed to get quite a chuckle out of that, but Max hushed her immediately.

"Georgette, how can you laugh at a time like this?"

"But, sugar—"

"Enough now," he said emphatically. "Be still."

Chester glanced at me knowingly.

"So," Max said, turning to us, "to what do we owe the pleasure of your—shall we say, unexpected—company?"

"We were just in the neighborhood, so we thought we'd drop in," Chester replied smartly. I was impressed by the quickness of his wit. I tried to think of a quick comeback, too, but it takes me a while to think of quick comebacks. By the time I was ready, Chester had already strolled into the bungalow, casually shaking out the rain from his hair as he went. I followed his lead, but when I shook the rain out of my hair, there was nothing casual about it.

"Harold, sugar," Georgette cried, "you're makin' it rain indoors."

"Oh, sorry," I said, sheepishly.

"Well, it was nice of you to stop by, anyway," she said then. "I guess." She looked with uncertainty at Max, who glowered at Chester and said nothing.

After an awkward silence, Chester spoke. "We

were sorry to hear about Louise. If there's anything we can do . . ."

"Aw, shucks," Max said, his face softening. "That's really big of you."

"I mean, if we can help you *out* in any way," Chester added with emphasis. He looked meaningfully at Max. Max averted his eyes and pawed at the ground.

"Oh, I doubt there's anything anyone can do," he mumbled. "We'll just hope she comes back soon, that's all. Meanwhile, I'll just have to bear my sorrow alone."

Chester nodded sympathetically at Max. "Of course," he said, "we understand." And then, under his breath, he muttered, "Save it for the judge."

"What about me?" Georgette asked. "I'll bear it with you, Maxy."

"Gee, thanks, Georgette."

I noticed Chester's face out of the corner of one eye. He was taking it all in.

"Well, I suppose you're right," he said. "There really isn't anything we can do. Just wanted to let you know——" He paused dramatically and spoke with great intensity. "——that we're here if you need us."

"Right," Max said, sticking out his jaw. I gathered that for a bulldog, a stiff lower jaw was the equivalent of a stiff upper lip for the rest of us.

The rain was letting up, a perfect excuse for us to take our leave. We raced back to Chester's bungalow.

"Well, I couldn't hear everything," Chester said, as soon as we were inside, "but what I did hear was pretty incriminating."

"What does that mean?" I asked.

"It means it's not the kind of stuff you'd want your mother to know."

"Oh."

Chester bathed himself as he continued. "It seems," he said between licks, "that our friends Max and Georgette are planning to escape."

"Really?" I asked. I could feel my eyebrows take on a life of their own.

"Really," Chester replied. "The first voice I heard was Georgette's. She was saying something like 'We have to stick together and everything will be all right.' "

"Wow!"

"That's what I thought. Then Max said, 'But what if we're caught?' and Georgette said, 'That's why we have to be very careful. We'll go when it's dark. First we have to find a way out . . .' And that's all I heard."

"That's too bad," I said.

"Yes, it is," Chester agreed. "Unfortunately, a certain party who shall remain nameless dropped me right at that moment."

"Oh," I said, swallowing. I decided not to respond further. "Well," I went on, "obviously Max and Georgette are the guilty ones. They murdered Louise and now they're planning their getaway. Gee, it's hard to believe it's really happening. It's like something you'd read in a detective story."

"Not so fast," Chester cautioned. "It doesn't look good for them. But I'm still not convinced they did it."

"You're not?" I asked in surprise.

"Not at all," Chester replied. "They're not the only ones with a motive. *And* there's still a big piece of the puzzle that doesn't fit. Until it does, I won't know for sure who the murderer is."

"What's that?" I asked.

"Well, Harold, I don't know about you, but I had a lot of trouble sleeping last night. Howard and Heather were howling so much, I don't think I slept at all. If anyone had walked across the compound, much less dragged a body across it, I would have known. But I didn't see or hear anything. All night long. Doesn't that seem odd?"

I had to admit that it did. "What do you make of it?" I asked Chester.

"I don't know what to make of it," he confessed.

"Maybe whoever did it didn't want to get wet, so they waited for the rain to let up," I suggested.

"But that would mean early this morning, when it was light already. Nope. It would have been too risky."

"Then it had to be last night."

Chester was deep in thought. "Yes," he murmured softly. "Yes, last night." Suddenly, his eyes lit up. I was aware that at that moment the rain stopped. It was very still when Chester uttered his next words.

"That last piece of the puzzle, Harold?"

"Yes?"

"It just fell into place," he said.

"Huh?"

"I just figured it out, Harold." His voice became louder and more excited. "I don't know why, and I don't completely understand how, but I know who did it. Without a doubt, I know who did it."

"You know who did what?" Taxi's voice said sharply.

Surprised, I turned to see Taxi, Lyle, Georgette and Max gathered at the door of Chester's bungalow. It was Max who spoke next.

"Taxi tells us you and Harold are saying he murdered Louise," he said.

"Nonsense," Chester replied immediately. Nothing seemed to faze him.

"He said he overheard you talking."

"He may have overheard us talking, but he never heard us say he murdered Louise."

"You believe that Louise was murdered?" Georgette asked, her eyes growing wide. "How can you say such a thing?"

"I say it because it's true," Chester replied matter-of-factly.

"Oh, come on, mate," Max retorted. "You have an overstimulated imagination, if you ask me. Just like Lyle. I've always said that about cats."

Lyle was outraged. "Don't put me in the same camp as Chester," he cried. "I may be crazy, but I'm not *that* crazy! I never accused anybody of murder. He's a troublemaker. String him up! That's what I say. Let's string him up!" Hysterical, he dashed off, I presumed in search of rope.

Chester stared coolly at the three who remained. "Yes," he said, "I know who murdered Louise. I need just a little more information, and when I have it, I'll prove my case."

Max began to laugh.

"Go ahead and laugh," Chester snapped, cutting him off mid-chortle. "Yes, my friend, laugh today, for tomorrow you'll know the truth. And then, perhaps, you'll never laugh again."

I noticed that Howard and Heather had come up behind Taxi and were listening to what Chester had to say. I felt myself trembling as I beheld the five pairs of eyes staring penetratingly at Chester. It was so quiet you could have heard a doggie-pop drop.

And then, all at once, Heather threw back her head and let out an ear-splitting howl.

"Aaaah-oooooooooooooooooooooo!" she cried. Gasps of shock went out from us all. She looked about her, an expression of great surprise on her face.

"So sorry," she said softly. "Just not myself. Oh, how embarrassing. I think I'd best—"

"—rest," Howard continued. "Yes, dear, I do think that's best." And off they went, their heads bobbing all the way back to their bungalows. We watched them go.

Then, without a word, Max, Georgette and Taxi followed, leaving Chester and me alone with each other and our thoughts.

I looked at Chester. A cool smile sat on his lips.

"How can you smile like that?" I asked. "Don't you realize what a dangerous thing you've done? Exposing yourself like that? Now the murderer knows you've found him out."

"Oh, I don't think I've done such a dangerous thing," Chester answered smoothly. He was quiet then, and I remember looking at him, hoping that he was right and feeling somewhere deep in my bones that he wasn't.

He was lost in thought for the rest of the day. In fact, the only time he spoke to me again was shortly before dinner.

"Just one word of warning," he said. "Keep awake tonight. The murderer may strike again. Remember: *do not sleep.* If you do, you may never wake again."

How it chills me to recall those words. Particularly when I think of them as Chester's last.

SEVEN

Good Night, Sweet Chester

I SHOULD have known something was wrong when tears fell on my breakfast. I looked up and saw that Jill was crying. She didn't say a word, but when she caught me looking at her, she burst into a fresh bout of sobbing. Shaking her head as if to deny something she knew to be true, she closed my door and moved on to feed the others.

I heard her move past Chester's bungalow and then I called out, "Chester, Chester." There was only silence.

"Chester," I called again. "Why is Jill crying?" Silence. "Answer me, will you? What's the matter? Cat got your tongue? Heh, heh, heh."

Again, no response. I was beginning to worry. But not so much that I let it stand in the way of breakfast.

When I looked up from my food dish, I saw that Jill was going back into the office. I knew it was risky, but I had to find out why Chester wasn't talking to me. I pushed up the latch to my door with my nose and cautiously crept over to Chester's bungalow.

A shadow fell across his door, making it hard to see inside.

"Chester?" I whispered. I strained my ears to pick up a sound. Any sound. I thought maybe he was still asleep and I'd hear his breathing. Or a rustle of movement.

"Chester!" I snapped impatiently. "Wake up!"

But then my eyes adjusted to the shadowy scene before me. I held my breath as I realized the truth.

Chester was gone!

Immediately my mind began searching for a logical explanation. He was out investigating, I told myself. He was . . . he was . . . But what

I saw next stunned me into the realization that not only was Chester gone, he might not be coming back.

The bungalow was entirely empty. No food dish. No water dish. No rug on the floor. Only a rag of a mouse hanging limply by its neck suggested that the place had once been inhabited.

I didn't know what to think then. I stood there, useless as a fire hydrant in a town without dogs, and felt the tears welling up in my eyes. Oh Chester, I thought, why didn't I listen to you? You told me to stay awake all night, and I didn't. I was so tired I fell asleep right away. And then *this* happened. It was all my fault.

Feeling thoroughly miserable, I turned my head away. And then I saw them. All the guests of Chateau Bow-Wow, their noses pressed against the fronts of their bungalows, were watching me. Their silent vigil reminded me of the scene the night before. I saw in their eyes the same look I'd seen when they'd stared at Chester, accusing him wordlessly of . . . of what? Of knowing too much, I realized. Yes, Chester had paid a price for his curiosity. And for his big mouth.

The sounds of Jill's renewed crying within the office shook me from my thoughts. Maybe Chester is sick, I thought, and they've taken him indoors. I decided to find out what I could by listening at the office window. As I crossed the compound, I thought of our eavesdropping on Max and Georgette yesterday, and a smile came to my lips. It was funny thinking of Chester's tail tickling my nose, of our falling into the mud puddle, of his saying to me—

And then I felt a lump in my throat, and I thought no more about it.

Placing my front paws on the windowsill and standing on my back legs, I was able to see inside the office. Harrison, his back to me, stood by the examining table. Jill sat in an old beat-up chair next to him. She kept dabbing her red eyes with a handkerchief. Chester, I observed, was nowhere in sight. I strained to hear as best I could.

"I can't believe it," Jill was saying, between sobs. "I just can't believe it."

"Neither can I," Harrison replied. "But it's the only explanation."

"How did it happen?" Jill asked. "That's what I don't understand. It doesn't make any sense."

"Sometimes life is like that," Harrison said, waxing philosophical. "Sometimes life just doesn't make sense."

"We're not talking about life, Harrison. We're talking about—"

"Yes, I know."

Jill stopped crying and heaved a huge sigh. After a moment of silence between them, she looked up at Harrison. "It's all my fault, you know. I did it."

"Of course you didn't, Jill," Harrison answered calmly. "You've got to stop talking like that. These things happen, that's all. It could have happened to anyone. Look, I make mistakes, too, you know."

"Maybe, but *I* was the one who cleaned out that part of the storage shed. I remember carrying that stuff out to the street for pickup. I just don't understand how it got inside the compound."

"Uh . . . well . . ." Harrison said.

Jill looked up at him. "What?" she asked.

"Nothing," Harrison answered quickly. His eyes flitted nervously from side to side.

"What were you going to say?"

"Nothing, really. I just—"

"Harrison . . ."

"Never mind, I don't want to upset you."

"I'm upset already. Tell me what you were going to say."

"Okay, if you insist. I was just remembering that when you came inside the compound, you were carrying that bag of garbage . . ."

"When Louise was barking, yes," said Jill, with a worried look. "And the bag broke. *That*'s how it got there." They both fell silent. "Harrison?" Jill said then.

"Yes?"

"May I take the rest of the day off?"

Harrison paused uncertainly. Then he said, "Of course you can. Why not? Maybe the rest will do you good."

"Yes," was all Jill said in response, and then she stood. She took off her smock and started toward the door to the front of the building. Turning back to look at Harrison (I could see her face clearly now and had to duck down so she wouldn't see me), she said, "How could it have gotten into Chester's food? Just tell me that."

This was the first I'd heard Chester's name, and I felt my stomach tighten. How could *what* have gotten into Chester's food? I listened carefully.

"I don't know," Harrison replied. "All I know is that I found the container near his bungalow, and when I tested his food—"

"Poison?"

"Poison."

Poison. The word went through me like an arrow.

Jill spoke again. "And now he's . . ."

"Gone. Yes," Harrison said.

"May I see him?" Jill asked.

Harrison stepped toward her. He put his arms out to take her by the shoulders. "Why upset yourself anymore?" he asked. "I'll take care of everything."

"And Dr. Greenbriar?"

"I'll call him. Don't worry. Just go home and rest."

What happened then I don't know. I dropped down from the windowsill, no longer caring about anything more I might hear or see. I'd heard quite enough. Slowly, I stumbled back to my bungalow. Everyone may have been watching me still, but I have no recollection of anything except the lump in my throat growing larger with every step I took. And the thought that my best friend in the whole world was gone. Poisoned. And all because he knew too much.

Back inside my bungalow, I curled up as tight as I could and fell into a deep sleep.

EIGHT

Harold X, Private Eye

I AWAKENED to the sound of cloth being torn. From the low growls that followed, I surmised that a game of Rip-the-Rag was in progress. Slowly, I opened my eyes and stared out into the bright sunlight. At last, the storm had passed, and from the sight of animals at play before me, it appeared that all was well with the world. Max, Georgette and Taxi tugged at what looked like an old towel. Heather sat sunning herself, while Howard dug at the earth in the far corner of the compound. Lyle was wrapped around a ball of some kind, kicking at it with his hind feet. The scene was so inviting that for one brief moment, I wanted to run outside and join in the play.

And then I remembered Chester. My heart sank. And the thought occurred to me: someone out there, some seemingly innocent frolicker, was really a cold-blooded killer. How could I play with a murderer? I asked myself. And who could it be? Who could it be?

I cast my eye over each in turn.

Georgette let go of the towel and, merrily darting back and forth, nipped at Max's ankles. Sure, I thought, she has reason to be happy. With Louise out of the picture, she's got Max all to herself now. He didn't seem so miserable either, I noticed. How quickly his grief had spent itself. Well, why not? After all, if he had bumped Louise off, no one but Chester knew. A little poison in Chester's food, and there was no more need to pretend. Soon he and Georgette would run away together. Everything was going according to plan. Why shouldn't he be happy?

And Taxi? I watched as he collided with Max's shoulder. He fell back onto the grass and rolled around, scratching his back. Max ran off with the rag, waving it in the air. Suddenly, Taxi lurched to his feet and, picking up the challenge, grabbed one end of the rag from Max. They tugged in opposite directions. How pleased Taxi must be, I thought, if he were the culprit. After all, he'd wanted so badly to impress Max, to be his best friend. And now, it appeared, he had given Max everything he could ask for . . . and more. And, in return, he'd gotten everything he'd wanted, too. It was not easy to forget Taxi's interest in murder by poison. How excited he'd been when he first mentioned it to Max and me. No, he might appear on the surface to be a little dumb, but Taxi was no dumb dog.

The sound of scratching drew my eyes to Howard. What was he doing, anyway? He seemed to be digging a hole. To bury a bone, I thought. Or perhaps something else. He kept looking furtively over his shoulder, as if he were afraid of being caught. My glance fell on Heather. How strange the two of them were. Perhaps Chester had been right, maybe they were werewolves. I vowed to keep my eye on them.

Suddenly, Lyle sprang up and attacked a leaf that happened to blow by in the passing breeze. "Gotcha, you little devil," he cried. "You thought you could escape the long arm of the law, eh? Well, take that. And that." And he bludgeoned the poor leaf into a fine powder. He was an odd-ball, no question about it. I remembered his threat to Louise. And then his words from the night before popped into my head. "Let's string him up!" he had exclaimed as he ran off. Lyle was just crazy enough, I concluded, to carry out his threats. Murder would be as natural to him as playing with a ball of yarn was to most cats.

Just then, the door to the office opened, and Harrison stepped outside, coming in my direction. "Hey, Harold," he called out cheerily, "it's about time you were up. You going to sleep all day?"

"Woof," I answered.

"Oh, yeah? What kind of thing is that to say?"

Frankly, I wasn't sure myself what I meant by it.

He opened my door. "Come on," he said, "it's

almost time for dinner. How about getting a little exercise?"

Leaving my bungalow, I observed Harrison out of the corner of my eye. He was whistling now. His cheeks were puffed out and red from the force with which he blew the melody (such as it was) through his lips. Gee, he seemed happy, I thought. There was a twinkle in his eye as he patted my head and said, "Good boy, Harold." From anybody else, such good cheer would have been normal behavior. From Harrison, it was definitely suspect.

What if he's the one? I thought. Maybe he's in cahoots with Dr. Greenbriar, as Chester once suspected. Maybe they're doing some kind of awful experiment in their laboratory and . . . A shudder went through me as I thought of poor Louise and Chester in the laboratory of a mad doctor. I didn't let myself think about it any longer.

Harrison went back inside, and I surveyed the scene before me. Georgette and Max had gone off by themselves, and Taxi was rolling on the ground playing alone with the remains of the towel. It was at that moment I decided to take matters into my own paws.

I remembered something Chester had once said to me when I had refused to go along with him to investigate another of his little hunches. I'd promised him I'd stay home and think about it.

"Sure, sure," he'd said, "you may *think* about it, Harold, but I'm the one who will *do* something about it."

"What do you mean by that?" I'd asked.

"Cats are doers. Dogs are not. That's what I mean."

"I think you may be overstating your case."

"Think what you will," he'd said as he'd walked away. "The fact is that *I* am the one who's trying to do something. While you, O passive pooch, wrap yourself around your food dish and do nothing."

Once more I felt the sting of Chester's accusation. Do nothing! I thought. I'll show him he's not the only one with a brain. And so, with gritted teeth and a sense of great determination, I set out to unearth the truth.

I decided to start with Taxi, and I figured I'd catch him off guard with a direct assault.

"What do you know, Taxi?" I queried.

Taxi looked at me blankly. Perhaps that had been the wrong approach. I tried again.

"How are you, Taxi?"

"Oh hello, Harold," Taxi said, as if seeing me for the first time.

"Some storm we've been having, eh?" I asked him.

"Oh, I'm all right, I guess."

"What?"

"Fine, thanks." There was a pause as Taxi and I looked at each other. "You asked how I am, and I'm telling you I'm fine."

"Oh. Yes. I see."

"How are you?"

"I'm okay, I guess."

"You're welcome."

"Huh?"

"Oh, I'm sorry. I thought you were going to say 'thank you.' "

"For what?"

"For asking how you are."

"Oh," I said, "I'm sorry."

"That's all right."

"Thank you."

"You're welcome."

I looked at Taxi a long time. Suddenly, I couldn't remember what I had wanted to ask him, or why. Knowing Taxi, I decided, was definitely one of life's more confusing experiences.

"You're probably wondering how I got the name 'Taxi,' " Taxi mumbled so softly that at first I thought he was talking to himself.

"Well, no, I wasn't really, I—"

"Then I'll tell you, Harold."

"Thank you," I said, wondering when the dinner bell would ring.

"You see, I was owned by these people in New York City who thought that when they took me out for a walk, it would be cute to call 'Taxi!' People who live in New York City think things like that are cute. It's the air pollution that does it to them, I think. Anyway, for a long time, whenever they called 'Taxi' I thought they were really calling a taxi, so I wouldn't come. And the taxi drivers thought they were calling a taxi, too, so they'd pull up. So all the time they were getting all these taxis they didn't want and taxi drivers were getting mad at them and meanwhile I was wandering off down the street 'cause I didn't know they were calling me . . ."

"What happened?" I asked.

"Oh, eventually I figured out that 'Taxi' was my name, but by then I think they'd gotten bored with the whole thing. They bought roller skates and gave me to their cousin who lives in town here."

"Air pollution is a terrible thing," I commented.

"Mmmm," Taxi murmured, as he rolled over on his back. Just then, I remembered why I'd started this conversation in the first place. Interesting, I thought, how neatly he'd gotten me off the track.

"Taxi, I want to ask you something."

"Oh, hello, Harold."

"Where were you on the night of . . . uh

. . . um . . . uh . . . last night?" I asked
forthrightly.

"Huh?"

"Your whereabouts last night, Taxi."

"My what, Harold?"

"Your whereabouts!" Taxi looked up at me as
if his brain had just gone out to lunch. *"Where
. . . were . . . you . . . last . . . night?"*

"Oh, why didn't you say so?" He paused for a
moment. Now, I had him! I could feel it. "In my
bungalow, of course. Just like everyone else. Why
do you ask?"

Oh, he was a slippery devil. But I wasn't going
to be fooled so easily. I thought how proud Chester would have been of my investigatory skills.

"The truth now, Taxi!" I said. "Tell me the
truth."

"Okay," he said.

"That's better," I replied encouragingly.

"I was in my bungalow."

"You said that already."

"I know."

"Why are you telling me the same story?"

"Because it's true. And you asked me to tell you the truth, didn't you, Harold?"

"Yes, I did . . ." I could feel myself beginning to falter.

"I'm sorry about Chester," Taxi said then in a voice full of sympathy.

"Me, too," I said, completing my falter.

"Want to play Rip-the-Rag?" he offered.

Downhearted, I began to walk away. "No thanks," I called back over my shoulder. "Maybe another time."

"Okay," Taxi called out lightly. " 'Bye, Harold." And he returned to his tug-of-war with himself.

Not feeling particularly encouraged by the results of my investigation thus far, I was almost ready to give up and go home when I saw that Howard had stopped digging and was now sitting next to Heather in front of their adjoining bungalows. As I approached, I watched their heads move up and down and couldn't help thinking how terrific they'd look on the back window ledge of an old Chevy.

"Good afternoon," I said.

They stopped talking immediately and stared at me as if they'd been caught chewing on a leg of the dining room table. Neither said a word.

I cleared my throat. "Uh . . . good afternoon," I repeated.

They glanced into each other's eyes. No one spoke for what felt like a very long time. In a tiny voice, Howard finally said, "Good afternoon."

There was a pause. I decided to plunge in.

"Where were you last night?" I asked.

"Not much in the mood for conversation at the moment, Harold old chap. Frightfully sorry. It's just that we're—"

"Now, now, now," Heather interjected crisply, cutting Howard off from saying another word.

I had no choice but to plunge right back out again. "Well, another time perhaps," I said.

"Yes, yes," Howard said with a crooked little smile.

"Another time," Heather said firmly. And then just to make certain I got the message, she added, "Goodbye, Harold."

"Goodbye," I said, walking away and muttering under my breath, "It was nice talking with you."

Fortunately, I had no time to brood further over my lack of success, for I saw that Max and Georgette were coming toward me. I felt a little nervous. After all, they were prime suspects, and I didn't want to blow my examination. I considered how best to approach them. Clearly, they were too smart not to recognize a direct attack. No, with them, I reasoned, I would have to be subtle. I would work my way into it slowly, craftily, never letting them suspect what I was up to.

"Beautiful day, isn't it?" I asked casually, as they stopped before me.

"Oh, yes," replied Georgette. She smiled sweetly.

"Right you are, Harold," Max added.

"Well, speaking of what a beautiful day it is, last night certainly wasn't, so where were you?" I was extremely impressed with myself. If only Chester could have been there, I thought, to see just how clever and subtle I could be when I put my mind to it.

"What?" Max asked, pretending to be confused.

I heard the dinner bell ring and saw Harrison making his rounds. Drat, what a time to be distracted by food. Just when I had them on the ropes!

I'd forgotten exactly what we were talking about, but I didn't let that stand in my way. "A likely story!" I snapped.

Georgette looked concerned. "Harold, do you think maybe you've been out in the sun too long?" she asked.

An interesting ploy, I thought, trying to make *me* look like the suspicious one.

"Harold, pal," Max said gruffly, "it's been terrific chewing the fat with you, but we've got to run. Chow time, you know what I mean?"

I do indeed, I thought. Any excuse to get away, eh? "Think about what I've said," I told Max and Georgette as they started to go. I wasn't going to let them off the hook so easily. "You know where you can reach me if you have anything you need to get off your chest."

Max gave me a puzzled look, just to keep me thinking he was innocent, no doubt. "Sure, mate," he uttered, "anything you say."

"Oh, Harold," Georgette said then, "there is something."

"Yes?" Ah, a confession at last.

"We're sorry about Chester."

I'll bet you are, I thought. Just like you were sorry about Louise. But "Thanks," was all I said.

"Hey, Harold, let's go," Harrison called out. "Soup's on."

As long as it isn't split pea, I thought.

AFTER checking my dinner out for any uninvited smells or tastes, I plunged in. I was starved, which was understandable considering the amount of energy I'd used up conducting a tough and un-yielding criminal investigation. The only thing that bothered me about it was that I'd unearthed no new evidence.

What I *had* unearthed was doubt. Doubt in my own mind that anyone at Chateau Bow-Wow was the culprit. Or indeed that a crime had taken place. Perhaps Chester had conjured the whole thing up in his twisted imagination. It *was* possible, after all, that Louise had run away, just as everyone had said. And it may have been just an accident that led to Chester's poisoning. Perhaps all of it, I reasoned, was the unfortunate result of Jill's carelessness.

It was then that I noticed the writing on the bottom of my food dish. The letters were smudged so that it was hard to make out what it said at first. Boy, I thought, the least they could do is serve dinner in bowls you can read. I was definitely going to complain about the service. I strained my eyes and looked into the depths of my bowl.

The last word was "now." I had no trouble reading it because it was the only one that wasn't marked up. After a moment's consideration, I could see that the first word was "Hello!" The end of that word was messy, but "Hello!" it was. Of that I was certain. Because of all the black marks, the three words in the middle were harder to decipher. But having hung out around Toby when he did crossword puzzles on the living room floor,

I was pretty good at working my way around black marks. So, finally, I was able to figure it out. With a great sense of accomplishment, I uttered my findings out loud.

" 'Hello! How's your tummy now?' "

Fine, thank you, I replied silently, although my eyes are a little out of focus.

I went to the water dish, thinking what a cute thing that had been for a food dish to say. Too bad it had been so hard to read though. I thought of what a time I'd had trying to make out the word "tummy." It was almost as if someone had tried to cross it out deliberately.

Suddenly, my ears went up. I lifted my head from the water dish. What if . . . ? I asked myself. What if someone *had* tried to cross it out?

Again, I studied the bottom of my food dish, but this time with a new intent. How could I have missed it? This wasn't an old, worn-out bowl, and these weren't random smudges. Someone was trying to tell me something.

Looking at it this way, I saw a new message emerge. "Hello!" became "Help." "How's" became "Howls." The third word was a little harder to make clear, but I finally read it as "out." "Tummy" had been smudged out entirely, and "now" was left as it was.

"Hello! How's your tummy now?" became

"Help   Howls   out   now "

The sky was getting cloudy. A low rumble of thunder made it clear that the day's sunshine had been only a brief respite from the storm.

Help howls out now, I thought, as I lay down to sleep.

"Help howls out now."

What did it mean?

NINE

And Then There Were Three

IT WAS useless trying to sleep. Even if I'd been able to get the message of the food dish out of my mind (which I wasn't), my eardrums were assaulted by Howard's and Heather's ceaseless caterwauling. It seemed worse than usual that night, with one taking up the howl as soon as the other had left off. With it all, the storm was again raging in full force, thunder and lightning exploding in the air like a giant fireworks display. In short, Chateau Bow-Wow was not exactly slumber heaven that night.

"Help howls out now." I turned the phrase

over and over in my head. I had already decided that "howls" referred to Howard and Heather. Someone was telling me to help them out. But who? And why? They seemed perfectly capable of taking care of themselves. The way they kept apart from everyone else, they probably wouldn't accept help even if it were offered. Unless—and here I stopped for a moment to consider this new thought—unless *they* had sent the message. Maybe they were saying, "Help *us* out now." Were they in trouble? Were they, in fact, the next victims?

A sudden crash of thunder startled me into the realization that it had become very still. For several minutes there had been no thunder. And no howling. Why? I asked myself. And then a flash of lightning revealed it all.

In that fleeting moment of illumination, I saw two figures scurrying across the compound. Howard and Heather are out, I thought. And then the words in the food dish took on a new meaning. What if, instead of "Help howls out now," it read "Help! Howls out now"?

A scene rapidly played itself out in my mind. Chester is eating his dinner. He looks up. Howard and Heather are staring at him through the wire mesh of his bungalow. He realizes that they have put poison in his food, and as he takes a last gasp of breath (I could feel the tears coming to my eyes as I imagined this part), he finds some way to scratch out the message on the bottom of his food dish, hoping that somehow it would reach me. A cry for help. A warning from beyond! That was it, I was certain.

Without giving a thought to what I'd do once I got there, I threw open my door and raced across the compound to Howard's and Heather's bungalows. Taxi must have seen me coming, because he called out, "Harold!"

I didn't answer.

"Harold, is that you? What are you doing? What's going on?"

I stopped dead in my tracks. Howard and Heather were gone.

"They're out again!" I cried. "On the loose!"

"What are you talking about?" Taxi asked. "Who's out?"

"Howard and Heather," I answered. "Have you seen them, Taxi? We have to find them before it's too late."

"Sure, I've seen them. Seems like I've seen everybody tonight."

"What do you mean?" I asked. "Who have you seen?"

"I just told you, Harold. Everybody. Well, everybody but you, that is. Until now, that is. Now, I've seen you, too. Boy, it's been some night. Try and sleep? Forget it."

"*Who* have you seen?" I demanded again.

"*Everybody!* First Howard and Heather were running around. I thought that was pretty silly. I mean, with the rain coming down like it is and all. Seems to me it's a good night to stay at home, you know what I mean?"

"Who else?"

"Oh, well, then Max and Georgette . . ."

"So they were out, too," I said under my breath.

"Yeah. I thought, boy, some night for a picnic. Then I got mad that I wasn't invited, so I went to the back of my bungalow and sulked."

"And Lyle?"

"I don't know if he sulked or not. He probably did, knowing him. But you'll have to ask him yourse—"

"No, no," I interrupted. "I mean, was he out, too?"

"Oh." Taxi paused for a moment to think it over. "Yes. No, no, I don't think so. Maybe. I'm not sure."

I glanced over at Lyle's bungalow. I heard him muttering to himself inside. And then I cast my eyes in the direction of Max's and Georgette's bungalows. They were both empty. Mystery upon mystery, I thought. What did it all mean?

I thought back to the message at the bottom of the food dish. If it read "Help! Howls out now," it might mean that Howard and Heather were the murderers and that they'd now killed Max and Georgette. Or if it read "Help howls out now," it could mean that Howard and Heather were next on the list of victims, that Max and Georgette were the killers and they'd struck again. Now they'd escaped, just as they had planned. My mind was spinning.

"Taxi," I said, scratching myself behind the ear.

"Yes, Harold?"

"What do you make of it?"

"Oh, I'd say it should let up by tomorrow morning."

"Huh?"

"I think it'll blow over soon. This is just a little squall. I don't think—"

"I'm not talking about the storm, Taxi," I said sharply.

"Oh."

"I'm talking about all these strange disappearances."

"I don't know what to make of it, Harold," Taxi said after thinking a moment. "But I'll tell you one thing."

"What's that?"

"I sure will be glad to get back home."

I looked around the compound. There were three of us left. Three out of nine who had started the week at Chateau Bow-Wow.

"So will I, Taxi," I said softly. "So will I."

* * *

BACK INSIDE my bungalow, I shook myself dry and lay down to think. I really didn't know what was left for me to do. Obviously, I'd been too late. Whatever the message had meant, Howard and Heather were gone, and there was no longer anything anyone could do to help. With a heavy heart, I shut my eyes and tried once again to sleep.

I shall never forget my dream that night. I was the only one left. In all of Chateau Bow-Wow, perhaps in all the world, I was the only one left. I went running from bungalow to bungalow, crying "They're gone! They're gone!" And then, from all around me, a terrible cry went up. It was like Howard's and Heather's howling, but echoing and coming from all directions. I tried to run from it. I ran in a big circle, round and round, attempting to escape the awful sound. "They're gone!" I cried again, as the howling reverberated in my ears. And then I felt myself being kicked. Over and over. It was Chester. Or the ghost of Chester. Kicking me and accusing me. "You blew it!" he snarled. "I tried to tell you, but you couldn't figure it out until it was too late. Boy, leave it to a dumb dog!" The kicking went on and on. It was so bad that it woke me up. "Chester!" I cried, thinking I was still in my nightmare.

"It's about time!" a voice replied.

I shook my head, trying to make clear if I was asleep or awake.

"Boy, Harold, nobody sleeps the way you do. Even for a dog, you're in a class by yourself!" I'd know that voice anywhere. And those insults! It could only be . . .

"Chester!" I cried.

"Well, give the little dog a big cigar!" he said.

There was no doubt about it. I was awake. And Chester was back.

TEN

Mystery, Mayhem and Mud

I COULDN'T believe my eyes.

"Was it all a dream?" I asked Chester.

"Of course it wasn't," he said. "Now, come on. We've got to move fast."

I was still blinking in disbelief when I heard a howl that sounded like the one in my dream. Echoing eerily, it sent a shiver all through me.

"Howard and Heather!" I exclaimed. "It's them, isn't it, Chester? They're the ones, aren't they?"

"Yes, yes, yes," he answered impatiently.

"It's been them all along, hasn't it?"

"Come on, Harold! Move!"

As I was pulling myself to my feet, I heard a voice call out, "They're gone!"

"Chester!" I cried in amazement, "This is just like my dream. The echo. The voice. Everything. What's happening? Who just said 'They're gone!'?"

"Harrison," he replied quickly, as he pushed against my hind legs (which were still sitting) with the top of his head. "No more questions, Harold. Just follow me. We've got to get the others."

"And help Harrison find Howard and Heather," I added, but Chester was already out the door and couldn't hear me.

By the time I found him, he was already scratching at the door of Lyle's bungalow.

Lyle was talking in his sleep. "Oh, yeah?" he was mumbling. "Says who? Think you're a tough guy, huh?"

"Psst, Agent 47X," Chester whispered.

Lyle's eyes popped open. He regarded Chester with a look of total befuddlement.

"Wake up!" Chester commanded.

Something inside Lyle snapped into focus. "What is it, Agent 37B1943X10YKLB97—" I think he would have gone on till morning if Chester hadn't cut him off.

"A secret mission. Follow me," he said.

Lyle flipped open his door and crawled out. He looked stealthily out of slitted eyes and kept low to the ground as Chester led the way to Taxi's bungalow.

"Don't let Harrison see you," Chester hissed back at us.

"But why?" I started to ask, when Chester cut me off with a sharp *"Sshhh!"* We continued creeping across the muddy compound until we arrived at Taxi's. He was wide awake and looked out at us as if he'd been half-expecting our arrival.

"Boy-oh-boy-oh-boy," he said in greeting. "Can't a soul get any sleep around this place? What is going on, anyway?"

"Ask Chester," I replied.

"Okay," Taxi said, and then with a start, he exclaimed: "Chester!"

"*Sshhh!*" Chester retorted.

"Chester!" cried Taxi again, but this time in a tiny voice. "You're back!"

"Yes, yes, I'm back."

"But how—"

"I'll explain later. Right now, we've got more important things to deal with."

"How do I know you're not a ghost?" Taxi went on. "Do something so I'll know you're not a ghost."

"How would it be if I bit your nose?" Chester hissed through clenched teeth. "Would that be proof enough for you?"

Taxi thought a moment. "Yes," he said then, "yes, I guess that would do it."

"Agent 35HBO7575NFL13YXX42—"

"Hike!" Taxi cried.

"What is it, Lyle?" Chester asked, turning his head.

"Can we get this operation underway? I was in the middle of a good dream."

Chester shook his head in dismay. "What a crew! I should have done this myself."

"Done what?" I asked. "I still don't under-stand—"

There was a crash of thunder and, in the accom-panying lightning, I could see Harrison standing several yards away. Chester noticed, too, and mo-tioned to us to huddle together and keep our voices down. Taxi crept out of his bungalow and put his head close to mine.

"Howard and Heather are somewhere nearby," Chester told us. "We have to get to them before it's too late."

"Help! Howls out now!" I thought.

"What should we do?" I asked, as the rain quieted to a steady drizzle.

"Just wait," Chester ordered.

"For what?" queried Taxi.

"For a sound that will tell us where they are."

Thinking he meant their howls, I was not at all prepared for what I heard next. Or for its sig-nificance.

My ears perked up as tiny yips resounded softly through the murmur of the rain.

"It's happened," Chester said softly.

"What has?" I asked.

"Sshh. Listen."

I did as Chester bade me, but what I was listening for, I didn't have a clue. The yipping sound continued, echoing as if from a great distance. And yet, I had the feeling it was coming from someplace very near.

"That's it!" Chester cried. "I know where they are! Let's go!"

At the very same moment, Harrison shouted, "I know where you are, you little devils! Now I've got you!"

Chester and Harrison both ran to the corner of the compound near Howard's bungalow. I was relieved to see that Chester no longer cared whether or not Harrison saw us. After all, if we were going to help him, he may as well know about it.

"Chester!" Harrison cried out, as he and my feline friend reached the same spot at the same time. "Where did you come from?" I imagined that it must have been quite a shock to Harrison's system to see Chester returned from the dead. But he appeared to be so determined to find Howard and Heather that he didn't dwell on it.

"Never mind," he muttered, as he began pulling at a plank of the back fence, "I'll deal with you later. Right now, I've got . . . to . . . get this . . . off." The plank, which was somewhat loose to begin with, tore off suddenly in Harrison's hands and fell to the side.

At first I couldn't see anything, but then Harrison shined his flashlight through the opening in the fence, and what I beheld on the other side amazed me.

There, inside the storage shed, their eyes gleaming in panic at the sudden intrusion, were Howard and Heather. A discarded rainpipe ran along the ground from where they sat to the opening in the fence. No doubt that accounted for the echoing effect of their howling, I reasoned. As for the yipping sound of moments before, that was quickly accounted for, too. For there, next to Heather, huddled five or six squirming newborn puppies. Their yips, no longer amplified by the rainpipe, were as tiny as they themselves.

In the glare of Harrison's light, Howard began to bark.

Harrison laughed. "Sorry, ol' boy," he said,

"but you're going to have to come with me."

"Jump him!" Chester shouted. "Taxi, go for his ankles. Harold—"

"But, Chester," I stammered, "I thought we were supposed to help Harrison find Howard and Heather. Weren't they the ones we were after?"

"Yes, yes, of course," Chester snapped. "But not because they're the murderers. Don't you see? Harrison's the one! And it's Howard and Heather he's been after the whole time!"

Well, I didn't see at all, of course, but I decided this was not the time for further discussion. Particularly not when I looked up and saw Harrison glaring down at me.

"What are you all doing here, anyway?" he uttered in a low, threatening voice. "Get out of here! All of you! Move!"

We sat, riveted to our spots. Suddenly, Harrison lunged at me. I didn't know which way to turn.

"Jump, Agent16IQ!" Lyle shouted in my direction, as he leaped onto Harrison's shoulders.

I jumped. Harrison lunged. And he landed, face first, in a big puddle.

"Mmmphhgrrux," he said (or something to that effect), as he lifted his head out of the mucky water. "Get off of me, you stupid cat!" He tried to shake Lyle loose, but Lyle was going nowhere.

"The game is up, NY7!" Lyle cried out. "Your spying days are over." He dug his claws in to get a firmer hold, and Harrison let out a yelp. He struggled to his feet; Lyle held on tight.

"Taxi!" Chester cried out. "The ankles! I'll join Lyle. And Harold—"

"Yes?" I asked. I wasn't very good at rough stuff, so I wasn't sure what I could do to be of help.

"Bark!" Chester commanded.

"But, Chester, you know how I hate the sound of barking."

"Bark!" Chester ordered again.

I wasn't sure what good it would do, but I did as I was told. Loudly, I barked. Howard joined in.

Chester jumped up onto Harrison's back and Taxi began nipping at his ankles.

"Hey, what's going on here?" Harrison cried. "Get off of me! Ouch!" Chester must have gotten in a good one. "What's with you animals all of a sudden? Ow, Taxi, get away from my feet!" Harrison kicked at Taxi, who fell over backwards.

"Are you okay?" I asked, concerned that he'd hurt himself.

"I'm fine," Taxi answered. He broke into a smile. "Isn't this fun?" he asked. And then he dove for Harrison's feet again.

"Break his thumbs!" Lyle was shouting gleefully. "We'll teach him a thing or two!"

"Attaboy, Lyle!" Chester said encouragingly. "Come on, Harold, what happened to the barking?"

Oh yeah.

"Woof! Woof!" I couldn't help thinking how dumb I sounded, but, unfortunately, a dog's vocabulary is limited. Just then, I heard a car pull into the driveway. Maybe "woof" wasn't so dumb after all; it seemed to have done the job.

The gate to Chateau Bow-Wow flew open, and Jill and Dr. Greenbriar rushed in. They were followed by Max, Georgette and—yes, it had to be, it was—Louise!

"Okay, Harrison, that's enough!" Dr. Greenbriar shouted.

Harrison froze to the spot. His eyes widened in amazement as his mouth fell open, and his flashlight fell to the ground. The light went out.

There was a long moment of silence, and then Jill's voice cut through it like a knife.

"Harrison, how could you?" she said at last.

Harrison mumbled something under his breath, as Jill and Dr. Greenbriar moved in closer to confront him face to face. Lyle and Chester hung stubbornly from Harrison's shoulders.

"I only hope, Harrison," Dr. Greenbriar said, "for your sake as well as theirs, that no harm has come to any of these animals."

"When I think of how I trusted you . . ." Jill interjected.

"How did . . . did you . . . how did you . . ." Harrison stuttered.

"Oh, I knew you were up to something after I called you tonight, Harrison," Jill answered. "You were so strange on the phone. Nervous and jumpy. I'd never heard you like that before. And then, well, I thought about how weird it was that you were here instead of home in the first place. I mean, *that* dedicated you're not."

"I never should have answered the phone," Harrison said weakly.

"Yes, that was your first mistake. And then on the way over here, we passed your house and found the dogs barking outside your window."

"I don't know what's going on," Dr. Greenbriar said, "but you and I have to talk, Harrison. First, I want to take a look at everyone and get them back into their bungalows. I'll check on Howard and Heather and the kids. If they're all right, we'll leave them where they are for the night. Harrison, wait inside the office until I come in. I want a full explanation. And then . . ." and here he paused dramatically, staring into Harrison's eyes, ". . . then we'll decide your fate."

Harrison hung his head as Dr. Greenbriar moved beyond him and through the opening in the fence. Jill stayed where she was.

"I just can't believe you'd do such a thing!" she said vehemently, her eyes connecting with the top of Harrison's unruly thatch of hair. "What got into you, anyway?" she demanded. "Was *this* how you were going to make a million dollars? By lying? And kidnapping?! And murder? And on top of everything, making it look like it was all my fault! I can't believe it, that's all! I just can't believe you're capable of such evil."

Harrison continued to stare at the ground, avoiding Jill's gaze.

"Well?" she asked after a moment. "Don't you have anything to say for yourself?"

Harrison shrugged and lifted his head slightly. In a soft voice, he uttered his defense. "You can't blame a person for trying."

Jill just shook her head slowly and watched as Harrison shuffled off toward the office door. Then, she moved away to join Dr. Greenbriar in the storage shed. Chester and Lyle jumped down from Harrison's shoulders. And Taxi came over to me with a piece of Harrison's sock hanging from his mouth. A souvenir of his night of bravery, no doubt.

When he reached the office door, Harrison turned back and sighed heavily. I almost felt sorry for him then and turned to Chester to tell him so.

"Don't waste your pity," Chester replied. "When I tell you about Harrison, you're not going to have such a soft spot in your heart for him."

Just then, Louise walked over to me. "Scott," she said to me softly. I wanted to remind her that my name was Harold, but she continued before I could say anything. "Scott, I know you have held out hope that we'd get together. But I am going back to Chip. He wants me . . . and, well, I am wanting him. I'm going to forgive and forget. No matter what has been between him and Liza. Forgive and forget, Scott, I hope you can understand." She walked back to Max's side.

Chester and I turned to each other.

"What terrible thing did Harrison do to Louise?" I asked in shock. "Mind control?"

"Worse," Chester answered. "Two days of afternoon television."

I looked back at Louise and a feeling of horror overwhelmed me. Chester was right. There could be no pity for Harrison.

ELEVEN

In the Days That Followed . . .

IN THE DAYS that followed, a calm fell over Chateau Bow-Wow. After that fateful night, the storm died down and was replaced by hot, sunny weather. Heather was moved indoors with her babies; and Howard, when he wasn't inside visiting, was proudly extolling the virtues of family life. He also handed out bones on which he'd written, "It's a boy . . . and a boy . . . and a girl . . . and a boy . . . and a girl . . . and a girl . . . and a boy." I was very moved by his gift. Chester was nauseated.

"Typical dog present," he grunted after Howard

walked away.

"What do you mean 'typical'?"

"You wouldn't catch a cat giving out used bones," he replied, as he rolled over on his back to bask in the sun. After a moment, he added, "Yuck! Just the thought of it—"

"Hello, Harold," a voice called out. It was Taxi, stopping by to chat. I told him I was sorry for thinking he might have murdered Louise and Chester, and he readily accepted my apology.

"Under the circumstances," he said to me, "it's understandable that you'd think I might have done it. After what I said about poison, I mean—"

"Yes," I replied, "and you seemed pretty upset about Max and Georgette, too."

"Well, I was a little jealous, I'll admit. But, Harold, do you really think I'd murder someone just because I was jealous?"

I was embarrassed that such a thought had ever crossed my mind. Chester, naturally, wasn't embarrassed in the least.

"It happens all the time," he said, "Besides, just because you look like you wouldn't hurt a fly doesn't mean you aren't capable. I checked into your file while I was being held in the office, and I found out a thing or two."

"Really?" Taxi asked in surprise. "What kinds of things?"

Chester just smiled.

"You read the files?" I asked.

"Yup," he said. "Harrison and I pored over every single one of them that evening. And let me tell you, there was some pretty interesting stuff in there."

I started to panic. I was hoping there was nothing in my file about the incident with the geranium. I mean, it had been in poor taste (and it tasted pretty poor, too) to eat Mrs. Monroe's favorite plant. I didn't sleep too well after that one, but whether that was from an unclear conscience or an unsettled stomach, I wasn't too sure.

Chester must have been reading my thoughts. He looked into my eyes with a knowing little smirk.

"Geranium?" I inquired innocently.

He nodded his head. Was nothing sacred? I

thought. Boy, you make one mistake in life and they never let you forget.

"There was also mention of the episode with Mr. Monroe's electric shaver," he added.

Boy, you make two mistakes in life and they never let you forget. That one wasn't really my fault anyway. Could I help it if I thought he was being attacked by an oversized bumblebee? It was a perfectly logical error.

"Clever of you to grab the shaver with your teeth and toss it in the toilet the way you did," Chester commented.

Taxi looked at me with a queer sort of expression on his face. I couldn't tell whether he was appalled that I had done such a stupid thing or appalled that he hadn't been as clever under similar circumstances. He just shook his head slowly and said, "You're some dog, Harold."

I decided to take it as a compliment. "Thanks," I replied.

"Yeah, you're some dog, all right," Chester joined in. "So clever you couldn't even figure out the message I sent you until it was too late."

"So it *was* from you," I said.

"Of course it was from me, you ninny. What did you think it was, a fan letter from Taxi here?"

Taxi looked puzzled. "What message?" he asked.

"Oh, just a little after-dinner reading I sent Harold," he answered.

"Huh?"

I was getting fed up. I had tried and tried to get Chester to tell me the whole story, but he kept pleading emotional fatigue. "Come on, Chester," I said. "Tell us what really happened."

"Okay, okay," Chester said irritably. "I'm still suffering from mental exhaustion, of course—"

"Would you like to suffer from physical exhaustion as well?" I asked between my teeth.

He picked up his tail with one paw and began to bathe it. "Boy, talk about impatience," he said.

Taxi whispered to me, "Is he going to tell us the story or take a bath?"

"I know Chester," I answered quietly, "and he always bathes his tail before he settles down. Don't worry."

"If you two boys in the back row will stop whispering," Chester said then, dropping his tail, "I'll begin." And so it was that I learned the true story of the strange events at Chateau Bow-Wow.

"AS I WAS eating dinner the other night," Chester began, "I felt myself growing drowsy. Oh, no, I thought, how could I be so dumb? I was so worried about staying awake that I hadn't even considered the obvious. And here it was, right before me."

"Here what was?" I asked. Chester stopped and gave me a look through half-closed eyelids.

"The food, Harold," he said.

"Oh."

"After all, we knew Louise hadn't eaten all of her dinner the night before. And we knew there was a good chance she'd been poisoned. By that time, I had figured out that Harrison was the culprit, so I—"

"How did you know that?" I asked.

"Patience, Harold. You can't rush a great mind."

"Oh. I'm sorry, Chester."

"That's all right. Now, where was I?"

"Something about a great mind," I said.

"Before that, you dolt."

"Oh . . . uh . . ."

"Oh, yes. So it stood to reason that if Harrison had poisoned Louise, he might pull the same trick on someone else. As I say, this thought didn't occur to me until I'd already eaten some of my dinner and was beginning to drift off. I tried to call out to you, Harold, but my voice was fading. You couldn't hear me."

I felt awful thinking of my poor, dear friend calling out for help in the bungalow next door and me being unable to heed his plea.

"Of course, you were slurping your food so loudly," he went on, "you wouldn't have heard me if I'd used a microphone and loudspeakers. Anyway, before I knew it, I was asleep."

"Then what happened?" Taxi asked.

"I slept."

"Oh," Taxi said, taking it in. "That makes sense."

"When I woke up, it was dark all around me. I didn't know where I was or how I had gotten there. After a while, my eyes made out a window, and with the help of the little bit of light coming through it, I could tell that I was inside a cage of some kind. I tried to undo the latch, but there was a heavy padlock on the outside. Seeing that there was no way to escape, I had no choice but to wait it out till morning.

"When I awoke again, it was light in the room, and I realized I was inside Greenbriar's office. Suddenly, Harrison's face appeared before me. I felt my heart pounding in my chest.

" 'Good morning, Chester,' Harrison said. I wasn't fooled by his pleasant tone of voice. 'I'm sorry, but I'm going to have to put you downstairs for a while.' And he picked up my cage, carried me down into the basement and left me there all alone. Now the thing is, I must have been near a heating duct or something because I could hear what was going on upstairs in the office. Jill had arrived and—well, it doesn't matter everything that was said. The important thing was—"

"I know," I said, interrupting. "I heard it, too. Harrison told Jill you were poisoned."

"Exactly," Chester said, looking at me with a puzzled expression. I smiled. Chester wasn't the only sleuth in the joint, and I wanted him to know it.

"Anyway," he continued, "he gave her the rest of the day off, came downstairs to get me and brought me back up to the office.

"Later, he took me out of the cage and put me on the examining table. I didn't know what was going to happen next. But I kept my eye on the window, which was open slightly, planning my getaway as soon as he came near me with any

funny-looking instruments. But he didn't do anything. Just sat down next to the table and stared at me.

" 'Are you the one?' he asked after looking me over from head to tail. 'I don't see what's so special about you.' Well, the insult aside, I found what he had to say very interesting. I wanted to know what he meant. So I began to purr. I sashayed over to him and bumped my head against his shoulder. I looked up at him with big, soft, mushy eyes, and just when I had him hooked, I got the purr going a little deeper in my throat so that it sounded like I'd just fallen in love. People are suckers for that stuff. Harrison was no exception.

" 'Aw, you're a nice kitty,' he said, patting me, 'but you don't seem very special.' I almost stopped purring at that, but remembered that I was after something. 'I was sure you were the one. Doc says you're special. I heard him tell your family. And your file has got some pretty interesting stuff in it. Still, you look like a pretty ordinary cat to me.' I wanted to bite him then, but resisted."

Knowing Chester, I had to admire his restraint.

"Well, then Harrison let out a big sigh and shook his head. 'Maybe I'm just not cut out for this racket,' he said. 'First I thought it was Louise. After all, she's pretty fancy-looking. But then once I got her home . . . I don't know . . . she didn't look so unusual. And *then* I looked back in her file and found out she's not even a purebred. So I figured I had the wrong one! Well, it's not so bad with her. I mean, I made it look like she escaped. I can just bring her back anytime I want. Meanwhile, she's not having such a bad time of it over at my pad. Watching TV all day, eating leftover Chinese food. What could be better? So, I went back to the files, and I read up on you, see? And I remembered what Doc said about you. And I figured *you're* the one. But, now, I don't know . . .' And he just stared at me some more, his face growing more and more perplexed.

"And then he said something that really frightened me. 'Too bad I made it look like you'd been poisoned. After all, I can't bring you back from the dead, can I? If you're not the one, we're both in trouble. Of course,' he added with a chuckle, 'you'll be in more trouble than me, but . . .'

"Well, I felt like running for the window then and there, but I was determined to see it through. What did he mean by 'the one'? Who was he after and why? I purred even more loudly. 'Hey, you're real friendly, aren't you?' he said. And then, reflecting back on his problems, he added, 'If only I'd heard the rest of that phone conversation.' He paused a minute and then looked me squarely in the eyes, as if he'd heard me asking him to explain.

" 'See, Chester, it's like this. I heard Doc saying to somebody on the phone that they shouldn't worry, that he knew how valuable they were and he'd take good care of them. But I never heard who he was talking about. I figured once I knew, I'd kidnap whoever it was, see? Make a mint, blackmail or something. You know? But how am I going to make a penny if I can't figure out who it is I'm supposed to kidnap?' Well, naturally, I knew right away who he was talking about."

"You did?" I asked.

"You did?" Taxi echoed. "Who was it?"

"And how did you know?"

"The thing about criminals is, no matter how smart they are, they're always just a little bit dumb. And that's where they get tripped up. Harrison hadn't even noticed that Greenbriar had said 'them.' So, obviously, he was talking about more than one animal. And since I knew that Howard and Heather were purebred wire-haired dachshunds (with the possibility of having been crossbred with werewolves, of course, which would only increase their value), I knew that they were the ones he was after.

"Later that afternoon, when Harrison was busy putting food into the dinner bowls, I made a run for the window, hoping to get out and warn Howard and Heather. Unfortunately, it wasn't open wide enough so I got stuck halfway through. Harrison pulled me back in and closed the window.

" 'Nice try,' he said to me, 'but you aren't going anywhere.' It was then that I had the inspiration to scratch out the message on the bottom of your food dish, Harold. I could only hope that you would be having one of your rare fits of intelligence when you ate dinner that night.

"Anyway, after he fed everyone, he put me back inside the cage and went home."

"But when . . ."

"I'm getting to it," Chester said. "He came back later that evening in a state of great agitation. 'I've got to find the answer,' he said. He pulled out all the files and started to look through them. I went into my purring number again, hoping he'd take me out of my cage so I could read over his shoulder. It worked. 'Just don't try to go anywhere this time,' he said. He needn't have worried. I was much more interested in finding out what more I could from the files. When he got to Heather's, there it was in nice, bold print: 'PREGNANT. DUE TO DELIVER SOON.' I looked at Harrison. How could he miss it? I thought.

"Then the phone rang. It was Jill, calling to remind him about the very thing we'd just read in the file. 'Yeah, I know she's going to give birth soon, Jill,' he said. 'Don't worry, it's a natural thing. Happens all the time.' Then she said something that stopped him dead in his tracks. He just stood there, his mouth hanging open. When at last he spoke, he said, 'Yeah, yeah. I heard you. Valuable. Of course, I know they're valuable. Don't worry. They'll be fine. Just fine.' He hung up the phone and ran for the door. 'That's it!' he cried. 'It's them! And all those little puppies in the bargain. I'll make a fortune selling them off!' He was so excited he ran out of the door without noticing what had become of me. Naturally, I was fast on his heels."

"And that's when you woke me," I said. It was more a statement than a question.

"That's when I *tried* to wake you," he answered. "It wasn't so easy."

Taxi looked dumbfounded. "He was going to sell Howard's and Heather's babies?" he uttered. "But what about *them?* What was he going to do with Howard and Heather?"

Chester shrugged. "Who knows? Maybe sell them, too. Maybe keep them locked up somewhere. Or perhaps, once he'd made his money selling the kids, dispose of the evidence."

"Wow," Taxi said, "that Harrison isn't such a nice guy."

"You can say that again," I concurred.

"Wow, that Harrison isn't such a—"

"Chester," I went on, "there are still some things I don't understand."

"For instance?"

"Well, for instance, what about Max and Georgette? If they didn't murder Louise, why were they planning to escape? Weren't they going to run away together?"

To my surprise, it was Taxi who answered. "If you hadn't been so busy suspecting everyone, Harold, you could have figured that one out a long time ago. They were planning to go look for Louise and bring her back. Max was convinced she'd run away because of him. Georgette felt terrible, too, so she suggested they go look for her together."

"You mean there was nothing between them?"

"No, of course not," Taxi said.

"Georgette is a bit of a flirt, that's all," Chester added, as if it had never been his idea in the first place that she and Max had murdered Louise.

So Harrison took Louise," I said softly, letting it sink in. "But how? You said you never saw anybody cross the compound that night."

"That's right," replied Chester. "That was what had me stumped. Then you said something that made it all fall into place. And that's when I knew Harrison was the culprit. Do you remember? You said that whoever did it would have gotten very wet."

"Yes, I remember saying that," I said, "but I don't see what that has to do with—"

"It made me think of the towels Harrison and Jill had used to dry us off."

"So?" I asked. "I still don't see—"

"Harrison wrapped Louise in a towel right while she was eating dinner and took her inside with him. No one saw her disappear. All they would have seen if they'd bothered to look was Harrison carrying a used towel into the office. And because it was already dark, no one even knew Louise was gone until the morning."

"And he made sure that her door and the gate were left open. Hmm, pretty clever," I admitted. "He really made it look as if Louise had escaped.

And that it was all Jill's fault. I was even beginning to think it was her."

"Sure. And do you remember that day they
were cleaning the storage shed?" Chester asked.
Taxi and I nodded. "Well, Harrison remembered,
too. And he remembered that Jill had dropped
some garbage inside the compound. He was able
to use that later when he told her he'd found a
container of rat poison near my bungalow. Just as
he wanted her to, she believed she'd dropped it.
And that her carelessness had resulted in my
death."

There was a long moment of silence as Taxi
and I tried to take in everything Chester had told
us. It was an incredible story. Even more incredible when I thought how close I'd come to never
seeing Chester again.

I looked at Chester and then up at the blue sky
above. The storm was over, I told myself, and
everyone was safe at last.

TWELVE

Howie

A T THAT MOMENT, I was attacked from
behind.

Thump!

I felt the blow between my shoulder blades.
"Help!" I cried out as I went sprawling onto my
belly.

"No mercy!" the voice above bellowed. "The
game is up. Your days are numbered. Resist, and
you'll walk the plank!" I recognized the voice.
Lyle had dropped by to say hello.

"Get him off of me!" I hissed at Chester, thinking he might know how to communicate cat-to-
cat.

"Agent 11½D!" Chester shouted. "Release
your captive!"

I felt Lyle's claws loosen. "Why?" he asked.

"You have the wrong dog," Chester shot back.

"Oh," Lyle muttered softly. He jumped off my back onto the ground before me. Calmly, he looked into my eyes. "Sorry about that," was all he said. And then he strolled off as if nothing had happened.

"There goes a great all-American twit," Chester said in tribute as he watched Lyle walk off. He shook his head sadly. "What a shame he has to be a cat."

"Now, I wouldn't have been surprised to find out Lyle was the murderer," Taxi commented. "I wouldn't put anything past him."

Chester shook his head again and sighed. "Lyle's had a rough life," he said. "You want some excitement? Read *his* file!"

"I think we've had enough excitement around here," I said to Chester. "And I think we can be grateful for one thing."

"What's that?"

"That with everything that's happened, no real harm has come to anyone."

I looked up and saw Max coming toward us. On his right was Louise. On his left, Georgette.

"Right!" he blurted as he came to a halt before us. "Just came over to see how you were doing, Chester. Must have been pretty tough for you, behind bars."

"I've been through tougher," Chester replied with typical modesty.

"It was a nightmare," Louise said dramatically. "I shall always forget my days and nights at the Chateau of Bow-Wow. How my heart it will ache when I am thinking of everything that has happened here. But, *alors,* in the end, everything is fine and we all live happily ever—oh, what is that word?"

"After?" Georgette offered.

Louise turned to Georgette and smiled sweetly. "Thank you, Camille."

Georgette started to correct Louise, then stopped herself. "You're welcome, sugar," she said instead.

Max smiled. "These gals have become great friends," he said happily. "Louise knows my heart belongs to her and her alone. And she knows that without Georgette, I never would have figured out how to break out of here and find her."

Georgette blushed. "Thank goodness Dr. Greenbriar and Jill came along when they did and heard our barking. By the way," she added, lowering her voice, "you can't imagine what a dump that Harrison lives in."

"Please!" Louise interjected. "I do not wish to be speaking of it. It was simply—" She pursed her lips as if searching for just the right word. "_abdominal!_" she proclaimed at last.

Well, it was close to the right word.

"Jogging?" Max suggested. I started to crawl away.

"No joggin', Max," Georgette replied. "How about Rip-the-Rag?"

"I have gotten it!" Louise announced. "Let us play Knock-Each-Other-Down!"

"Good!" Max snorted. "You fellows want to join us?"

"Maybe another time," Chester said. "Tennis elbow."

"Harold?" Max asked, turning to me.

"Uh, no thanks," I replied. "Coward cramps."

"I'll play," Taxi said brightly.

"Right! Let's go then."

Chester and I watched as the four of them hurried off into the distance to play Knock-Each-Other-Down. Before they had gotten too far, Louise ran back and whispered in my ear.

"Barry's been hitting the sauce again," she uttered. "I didn't want to tell you in front of the others. You have no idea what it's doing to Marcia. She's making a fool of herself over Ron. And all because of you, Todd." Todd? "It's no good, can't you see? How many times do I have to tell you? No, no, don't say anything. Just remember: when this nightmare is over, I'll still have Mike. All you'll have is a pocketful of memories and lint." She sobbed and ran off to join the others.

I turned to Chester. "You know what I said before?"

"What's that, Harold?"

"About no harm coming to anyone?"

"Mm-hmmm."

"Forget it. I only hope there's a cure for day-time television."

Howard howled in the distance. "Kids are great!" he called out, with a wink in our direction.

"Harold?"

"Yes, Chester?"

"This place is a loony bin."

"Yes, I know, Chester."

"I want to go home, Harold. I don't know how much more I can take of Lyle and Louise and Taxi and that crazy werewolf."

"Wait a minute, Chester," I said, "do you still believe Howard and Heather are werewolves? They've probably been acting strangely because they were nervous about having their babies."

"Werewolves can't get nervous about having babies?"

I had to admit the thought hadn't occurred to me.

"Uh-uh," he went on. "Nothing will convince me that they couldn't be part dachshund and part werewolf. Stranger things have happened." Howard let out another howl. "Besides, just listen to that. If that isn't the call of a werewolf, nothing is. No, I just want to get out of here. That's all I care about. Get me home, where I'll never have to listen to that terrible sound again."

I was about to answer him when the gate flew open and Toby and Pete bounded into Chateau Bow-Wow. As soon as he saw me, Toby came running in my direction.

"Harold!" he cried, throwing his arms around my neck. Boy, was I happy to see him! I started drooling like crazy.

"Chester!" Toby squealed, as he swooped the cat up off the ground and hugged him. Chester showed how overjoyed he was by not having a fit.

"Hey, guys," Pete said coolly.

"Boy, did we have a neat vacation," Toby said excitedly. "Wait'll I tell you about it."

"Yeah," Pete joined in. "Dad lost our travelers' checks and everything. Just like on TV."

"Yeah, and then we had a flat tire, and Dad had forgotten to put the spare back in the car before we left home, so we had to sit in the rain until the tow truck came."

"And then we were on this picnic and Dad fell out of the tree and now he's wearing this cast, see——"

"Yeah, and it's real neat, Harold. I wrote my name on it and everything."

"Me, too!"

"Anyway," Toby said, "sorry you had to be stuck *here* the whole time. I'll bet it was real dull."

Chester and I exchanged knowing glances.

"But now we're going home, boy. Come on, let's get your things."

What things? I wondered. I didn't remember having packed a toothbrush.

"Wait a minute," Pete said, "let's go ask Dad about you-know-what first."

"Oh, yeah, I forgot," Toby replied, dropping Chester to the ground. "We'll be back, you guys. Oh, here, Harold, here's a chocolate cupcake I brought for you. With cream in the center." And off they ran. The cupcake was a little smushed, which made sense since Toby had been carrying it in his back pocket. But it tasted delicious, especially after seven days of chocolate deprivation. That Toby was really a good kid.

A few minutes later, Dr. Greenbriar and Jill came out of the office door. I felt the blood pumping through my veins as they approached.

"I think the judge handled it very well," Dr Greenbriar was saying, "don't you?"

"Mm-hmm," Jill replied. "It might set Harrison straight after all. Even if he doesn't continue, a year of college can't hurt anybody."

"Pretty smart sentence, all right," the doctor said, smiling. "But what I liked best was the job he came up with for Harrison. To pay for school."

Jill smiled now, too. "Yes. Working at the zoo. I think that should suit Harrison just fine."

They laughed at the thought. I didn't think it was so funny. What if he tried to steal an elephant?

"Well, you boys are going home," Jill said, leaning toward us. "You must be glad about that, aren't you?"

"Bet your boots, sweetheart," Chester uttered under his breath.

We walked toward the gate, and we never looked back. We were going home at last.

MR. MONROE stood by the end of the station wagon, waving his good arm in our direction.

"Hey, Harold! How ya doin', Chester?" he called out.

Mrs. Monroe cooed her greetings, and then Pete and Toby came running over to us. I noticed that Toby was carrying something small in his arms.

"Harold! Chester! Wait'll you see the surprise we have for you," he sang out. I looked up and saw that he was carrying a little brown puppy. Chester's eyes went berserk. "Guess what!" Toby continued. "There were puppies born here a few days ago and one of them was the . . . uh . . . what'd ya callit . . ."

"The runt of the litter," Jill said helpfully.

"Yeah, right. And we're getting to keep him. 'Course, he has to stay with his mom for a while. But then we get to bring him home to live with us. Dad said we could, right, Pete?"

"Right," Pete chimed in. "And *I* got to name him."

"Yeah, but it's a good name anyway."

"Yeah, see," Pete went on, "the puppy's

father's name is Howard. So I named the puppy Howie."

Chester and I stared at Howie. He looked into my eyes, then into Chester's. And then, lifting his head slightly, he let out a tiny, tiny howl.

"*aah-ooooooooo.*"

"Gee, that's neat," Toby said.

"Yeah, neat," echoed Pete.

I turned to Chester and commented, "Before you know it, he's going to sound just like his mom and dad."

But Chester didn't hear me. He'd fainted dead away.

CHATEAU Bow-Wow was an adventure, and I suppose in some ways, Mr. Monroe was right: adventure *is* good for the soul. But what I like best about adventures is that they come to an end.

It's fall now, and I'm glad to be home. Fall means long walks in the woods with Mr. Monroe and Pete, late-night snacks of roasted chestnuts and pumpkin pies with Toby, and rolling in the leaves with Howie. Oh yes, Howie is living with us now. And since it's his first fall, there's a lot I have to teach him.

Of course, Chester is sharing in his education. Right now, he's teaching him how to meditate. Even as I write, I can hear them in the living room.

"*Ommmmm . . .*"

"*Omm-oooooooooooooooooo . . .*"

"No, you dumb dog. *Ommmmmm . . .*"

"*Omm-ooooooooooooooooo . . .*"

"Not 'ooooo,' you numbskull, '*ommmmm,*

OMMMMMM!' Can't you hear the difference? Don't you want to learn? Meditation is good for you. It'll make you mellow. Keep you cool. Like me. Don't you want to be like your Uncle Chester? Howie? Howie! Come back here! Where are you going? Get down from there! No, no . . . not the—Harold!"

Excuse me. I think I'm needed in the living room.

"Harold, get in here! I'm not a nursemaid!"

"In a minute, Chester!"

"He's going after the geranium! He's— he's—"

"He's what, Chester?"

"He's eating the geranium!"

"Coming, Chester!"

Well, I've got to go. It was quite an adventure, but when all is said and done, there's no place like . . .

"*Ommmmmmm . . .*"

What's next for Bunnicula, Harold, Chester, and Howie?

Here's an excerpt from the next adventure,

The Disappearance

IT WAS NOT a dark and stormy night. Indeed,
there was nothing in the elements to fore-
shadow the events that lay ahead.

Chester, Howie and I were gathered on the
front porch for a bit of post-dinner snoozing. I
was stretched out on my back, my paws dangling
at my sides, thinking of nothing more than the

meal I'd just eaten and the chocolate treat I hoped might still lie ahead. After all, it *was* Friday night, the one night of the week Toby was allowed to stay up to read as late as he wanted. And that meant snacks. Snacks to be shared with his old pal, Harold. That's me.

Chester, curled up on an open comic book nearby, purred contentedly. Only Howie, who was growling as he chewed vigorously on a rawhide bone, seemed unable to relax. But all that high-strung energy was natural, I suppose, considering he was still just a puppy.

"Boy, this is the life, huh, Uncle Harold?" Howie asked between growls.

"Mmph," I replied with as much vigor as I could muster. Which wasn't much. After all, I *wasn't* a puppy anymore and had used up most of my energy long ago. I listened to the sound of children playing down the block somewhere.

"There's nothing like hanging out on the porch after a good meal," Howie went on enthusiastically. He lifted his quivering nostrils to the air and sniffed rapidly.

"Ahhh! Smell that night air. Mmm, what's that? Somebody's having a . . . a what'd ya call it? What is it when they cook outside, Pop?"

Chester raised an eyelid. "A barbecue," he said with a yawn.

"Oh, yeah. Gee, I have so much to learn. But you and Uncle Harold have taught me a lot already." He gazed admiringly at Chester. "Thanks, Pop," he said.

Chester raised his other eyelid and shook his head. He turned his gaze from Howie to me.

"Why does the kid insist on calling me 'Pop'?" he asked. "I'm not his father. I'm not even a dog. If anyone around here should be his 'pop,' it should be you, Harold. Dogs of a feather should stick together and all that."

Howie chuckled. "That's a good one, Pop. 'Dogs of a feather . . . ' I'll have to remember that one."

I didn't even attempt to answer Chester's question. After all, Chester, who doesn't hold dogs in particularly high regard, did seem an odd choice of a father figure for a young pup. But Howie, who had recently come to live with us, had formed his attachment right away, and there was no breaking him of it now.

"Too bad the rabbit can't come out here, too," Howie went on with a nod toward the living room. "It's not fair, his having to be cooped up inside that cage all the time."

"I'm afraid that's a rabbit's fate," I said. "At least for a domesticated one. Though I must agree with you, Howie; I feel sorry for Bunnicula, too."

"Save your sympathy," Chester muttered. "Bunnicula is no ordinary rabbit. If he ever got out . . . and let's not forget that once upon a time he did, Harold . . . he'd only stir up trouble."

"Are you still convinced—" I started to say, but stopped myself, not wanting to alarm young Howie with Chester's theories of Bunnicula's true identity.

Chester looked mildly surprised. "Of course, I am," he replied. "Can there be any doubt? You saw the evidence yourself, Harold."

Howie looked back and forth from Chester to

me. "What are you two talking about?" he asked.

"Oh, nothing. Nothing." I thought of the cuddly little bunny-rabbit who'd become my friend, of the hours we'd spent snuggling in front of crackling fires on cold winter nights, of the time I'd saved him from Chester's attempt to starve him to death.

"That rabbit is a vampire," Chester said matter-of-factly.

Howie's head jerked up. The rawhide bone tumbled down the front steps. "What? A vampire?" He gasped. Then, after a moment's reflection, he asked, "What's a vampire?"

I felt obliged to step in and save Howie from the seamier facts of life.

"A vampire," I explained, "is the person who calls the rules during a baseball game."

"Don't confuse the kid," Chester said, bathing a paw. "And don't be such a Pollyanna." Turning to Howie, he said, "A vampire is a creature, once dead, who sucks the blood out of other living beings in order to live."

Howie's eyes widened in amazement.

"Wh . . . wh . . . what?" he stammered.

"So far, our friend Bunnicula hasn't attacked people," Chester went on calmly, "or cats or dogs for that matter. But he has drained the juices out of vegetables, turning them ghostly white. He came to live with us when our family . . . "

"One night the Monroes went to the movies," I said, picking up the story, "and found Bunnicula lying in a dirt-filled box on one of the seats."

"Don't forget which movie," Chester interjected.

"*Dracula*," I conceded, "but that doesn't mean—"

"Nonsense. In this case, everything means something. Don't you think it's significant that shortly after Bunnicula's arrival the vegetables in the kitchen started turning white? And wasn't it strange that they did so during the night, the only time Bunnicula wasn't asleep? Wasn't it stranger still that he could get out of his cage by his own powers? Without even undoing the lock? And what about those marks found in the drained vegetables? Two tiny holes that matched up perfectly with the rabbit's oddly-spaced teeth . . . or should I say, fangs?"

"I know, I know," I said impatiently. "We've been through all this before. But I'm still not convinced—"

"Nothing will ever convince you, Harold. I wouldn't be surprised if that bunny's got you in his powers. Listen, Howie . . . "

"Yes, Pop?"

Chester rolled his eyes and went on. "You can't listen to Harold on this one. He's too much of a goody-two-shoes. And the Monroes . . . well, what can I say? People are, alas, people, and, as such, woefully in the dark much of the time. They never had a clue what was going on. I was on the verge of destroying the vampire bunny once and for all, saving this town and all its inhabitants from his evil clutches, when the Monroes whisked him off to the vet and got him put on a liquid diet. Since then, he's had no need to suck the juices out of vegetables. A blender does all the work for him. Modern technology has once again saved the day. But . . . " and here Chester furrowed his brow ominously, "you can take the rabbit out of the vampire, but you can't take the vampire out of the rabbit."

"Huh?" I inquired.

"I don't get it," Howie said, scratching behind his ear with his back paw.

"You can take the—oh, never mind. What I'm trying to say is that I still believe if, for any reason, Bunnicula were deprived of his liquified vegetables, or had the opportunity to run away, he'd be back to his old tricks in no time."

Howie was so aroused by Chester's story he was panting slightly. "Wow," he said, trying to catch his breath, "and all this time I thought he was just a nice little bunny."

"He *is* a nice little bunny," I asserted, feeling the need to defend my friend. "Don't listen to Chester."

"Don't listen to Harold."

"Chester," I said.

"Harold."

"Pop, Uncle Harold," Howie barked. "Stop arguing. You're confusing me. I think I'd better run out and chase a car to clear my mind. Excuse me."

Howie started down the steps when Mrs. Monroe appeared at the door.

"Hello, boys," she said warmly. "I was wondering where you'd disappeared to. Howie, come back here. I've told you not to run out into the street."

"Rats," Howie muttered under his breath. He turned his face up toward the door and began whimpering.

"Now, that won't do you any good. Come on," she said, "it's getting late. Time to come in for the night. We're all going to bed."

Howie and I, being the obedient dog-types that we are, started for the door. Chester, a cat, lingered on his comic book, looking up at Mrs. Monroe with singular disinterest. She went over and picked him up. "Let's go, you little cutie," she cooed. "Sleepy-time."

Chester grimaced. " 'Little cutie,' 'sleepy-time,' good grief," I heard him mumble.

We entered the living room to find Toby and

Pete, the Monroes' two sons, staring into the television set as if they'd been hypnotized. I went over to Toby's side to see what it was all about.

"Gotcha!" Toby yelled suddenly, making me jump.

Pete bounced and twitched all over the floor as he frantically turned some dials back and forth and little blobs of light darted all over the screen. Weird noises—squawks and beeps and screeches—emanated from inside the television.

"I think our TV's possessed," I whispered to Chester, who'd jumped down from Mrs. Monroe's arms to join us.

"Don't panic, Harold," he reassured me. "I'll take care of it."

Slowly, he skulked across the floor, his eyes never straying from the flecks of light that dashed about maniacally on the screen. Every time two of them collided, another hideous screech was heard. When that happened, Chester's head jerked, his eyes widened, and a little more hair shot up along his back.

Suddenly, he pounced. With his paws racing

madly across the screen, he tried to catch the screaming specks of light.

"Chester!" Pete yelled. "Get out of the way."

"Yeah, Chester," Toby joined in. "Come on, you're ruining the game!" I was a little surprised at Toby, who was usually more patient than his brother. He now seemed as transformed as Pete by this strange new enterprise of theirs.

"All right, boys," Mrs. Monroe said, touching them lightly on the tops of their heads, "that's enough Star-Thrower for tonight."

"Star-*Eater*, Mom!"

"Yeah, Mom. Jeez."

"Star-Thrower, Star-Eater, whatever. It's time to call it quits and get to bed. Toby, you want time to sit up and read, don't you?"

"Yeah, I guess," Toby said. "Chester!" Chester was still busy trying to catch the elusive stars. "Just one more game, Mom. Okay?"

"No, it's not okay. Robert."

Mr. Monroe put down the book he was reading in a chair nearby. "You boys have a big day tomorrow," he said. "I think you'd better get some sleep. You heard your mother—no more Star-Catcher."

"Star-Eater, dear," Mrs. Monroe said. "I'm going to count to three. One, two . . . "

"Okay, okay," Pete said, and with a click the stars disappeared from the television sky. Chester, his front paws still stretched out on the screen, looked dazed.

"Everybody to bed. Now."

"Okay, we're going." The boys started up the stairs.

I planned to follow when suddenly I noticed Howie run up to Chester and whisper excitedly.

"Pop! Pop!"

Chester kept blinking his eyes at the television as if trying to figure out what had happened.

"What, kid?"

"Pop, what you said about Bunnicula. Your warning . . . "

"What about it?"

I glanced over to the rabbit's cage.

"Chester!" I gasped.

Chester dropped down and looked at us.

"What's the matter with you two?"

Howie, barely able to contain himself, blurted out, "The rabbit's gone! Look, he's not in his cage!"

With a start, Chester looked at the empty cage sitting on the table by the window.

"Where do you suppose he is?" I asked.

"Quick," Chester commanded, "to the kitchen!"

"Where are you off to in such a rush?" Mrs. Monroe asked as we brushed by her legs. "You were just fed. I'm afraid no more food has miraculously reappeared in your dishes."

That's too bad, I thought, as we tumbled through the swinging kitchen door and skidded to a halt on the linoleum inside.

All was quiet. The refrigerator door was closed. A bowl of fruit sat undisturbed on the kitchen table. We listened attentively for breathing, or hopping, or whatever noises rabbits make when they've run away. There wasn't a sound.

"Gee, Pop, he's not here," Howie said.

Chester looked wildly about, his mind clicking away all the while. "We've got to warn the Monroes," he said at last. "Come on."

We dashed back into the living room. The boys had already gone upstairs, and my thoughts strayed to Toby, who was no doubt already settling into bed with his latest book and an array of snacks. If I didn't hurry to help him out, he'd be forced to eat them all by himself. I headed for the stairs. Chester grabbed me by the tail.

"Where do you think you're going?" he asked in a somewhat garbled voice.

"I'm just hearkening to the call of chocolate," I replied.

"Well, hearken to this before you go anywhere," he said. "We've got to alert the Monroes to what's going on. Now, you and Howie start whimpering. I'll jump up on Bunnicula's cage."

"Well, all right," I agreed somewhat reluctantly. "For Bunnicula's sake."

Mr. Monroe was turning out the lights. Mrs. Monroe stood at the bottom of the stairs ready to go up. A pile of clothes was in her arms. Howie and I ran to her side and whimpered pathetically.

"What's the matter?" she asked, her voice full

of concern. "Do you want some water?" She turned to her husband. "Robert, why don't you check their water dishes before coming up? I want to start folding this laundry."

I noticed that Chester had jumped up on the top of the cage, but as that part of the room was darkened already, no one paid any attention. Mrs. Monroe went up the stairs and Mr. Monroe into the kitchen. Chester jumped down.

When Mr. Monroe reentered, he stood looking down at us, shaking his head. "I don't know what your problem is, fellas," he said, "but you've got plenty of water." Once again, I started to whimper as Howie tugged at Mr. Monroe's pants leg. Chester, meanwhile, began hopping around the living room floor, looking as if he was trying to make his way over a patch of hot tar. Mr. Monroe just smiled at him. "Well, Chester, it looks as if you're still full of energy. Too bad we can't let you out. Good night."

He patted each of us and went to bed.

"Gee, Pop, are you okay?" Howie asked. "Can I help?"

"You can help by not being so dumb," Chester muttered, a look of disgust on his face. "I was trying to be a rabbit."

Howie became confused. "Why would you want to be a rabbit?" he asked. "Aren't you happy being a cat?"

I moved toward the stairs, the lure of crinkling cellophane (covering, I hoped, chocolate cupcakes) too strong to resist. Chester called after me.

"Harold, take the kid with you, will you? I've got to plan my strategy."

"I want to stay with you, Pop," Howie said.

Chester groaned.

"What strategy?" I asked.

"We've got to find that rabbit and return him to his cage before it's too late."

"Too late for what?" I asked. "I'm concerned about Bunnicula, too, but—"

"It's not the rabbit I'm worried about," he said. "It's *us,* you fool. I shudder to think what could happen in one little night with that bunny on the loose."